THE DAYS OF
LAURA INGALLS WILDER

G·O·O·D
NEIGHBORS

Also by T.L. Tedrow

Missouri Homestead
Children of Promise
Home to the Prairie

BOOK THREE

GOOD NEIGHBORS

T. L. TEDROW

SCHOLASTIC INC.
New York Toronto London Auckland Sydney

Illustrations by Dennas Davis

ISBN 0-590-47612-2

12 11 10 9 8 7 6 5 4   5 6 7 8 9/9

Printed in the U.S.A.   40

First Scholastic printing, January 1994

To my pretty wife Carla and our younguns,
C.T., Tyler, Tara and Travis.

May we never forget the magic of childhood dreams which
is really what being young at heart is all about.

And to my good friends at Thomas Nelson,
for making these dreams come true.

CONTENTS

FOREWORD

Laura Ingalls Wilder is known and loved for her pioneer books and the heartwarming television series based on them. Though much has been written about the old West, it was Laura Ingalls Wilder brought the frontier to life for millions of young readers.

The American West offered a fresh start to anyone brave enough to face the challenges. These people tamed the frontier, crossing the prairie in wagons carrying furniture, seeds, and children, looking for a place to build a new life. They went west to raise families, build farms and towns, churches and businesses. They went knowing they would face hardship and danger, but that those who survived could build a future to offer their children.

Laura Ingalls's adventures did not stop after she married Almanzo Wilder. She went on to become a pioneer journalist in Mansfield, Missouri, where for sixteen years she was a columnist for the weekly paper *Missouri Ruralist*.

Laura Ingalls Wilder, a self-taught journalist, always spoke her mind. She worked for women's rights, lamented the consequences of war, and observed the march of progress as cars, planes, radios, and new inventions changed America forever.

While this book is a fictional account of Laura's exploits, it retains the historical integrity of her columns, diary, family background, personal beliefs, and the general history of the times in which she lived. However, any references to specific events, real people, or real places are intended only to give the fiction a setting in historical reality. Names, characters, and incidents are either the product of my imagination or are used fictitiously, and their resemblance, if any, to real-life counterparts is purely coincidental.

—T. L. Tedrow

CHAPTER 1

FIRST SNOW

The air was so cold that Laura could see her breath in the light filtering through the frozen crystal patterns on the windows. Thinking the quilt had fallen off the bed, she was too cold to sleep and too cold to get up.

Wrapped in a thin sheet that was no protection from the frosty air, Laura tried to find the quilt with her fingers. They moved across the bed, tapping and touching.

The quilt wasn't on the floor and wasn't at the foot of the bed. Laura patted to the left and right, trying to find the thick patch quilt that her grandmother had made for her. She lifted the sheet, intending to hurriedly grab a blanket from the cedar chest. However, when the chilly air slipped down her back like an icicle, she wrapped back up in the sheet and lay there shivering. Her fingers continued their search.

Near the other side of the bed, she finally felt the edge of the quilt. She tugged at it slowly, but it wouldn't move an inch. Grabbing a corner with her fingers, she gave it a tug. The only thing that gave was a bellowing snort from her husband, Manly.

Laura lifted her head off the pillow and looked over. Manly was wrapped up like a bear in the quilt, snoring contentedly. His breath was steaming out like a train engine running through a winter's night. "Manly. Manly, give me some of the quilt," she whispered.

"Wha—, wha—, what?" he stammered, half-awake.

"I'm freezing! You're hogging the whole quilt!"

"Here," he said, giving her just enough quilt to cover her big toe. "Now let me go back to sleep, will ya?"

Laura looked at the meager portion of quilt he'd given her and complained, "Come on, Manly. It's cold." But he had already drifted off to sleep. "Thanks for nothing," she said quietly. She looked at him in exasperation. He was snoring louder than ever. The windows rattled with the wind, sending a shiver down her back. *The coal heater must have gone off in the night,* she thought to herself.

This time Laura pulled the quilt and pushed Manly at the same time, hoping to get her fair share before he woke up. At that exact moment, however, Manly decided to roll over toward his edge of the bed, and with Laura's little push, he fell off!

The sound of Manly hitting the floor was magnified by the silence of the cold room. Laura wrapped herself up in the quilt, waiting for the scream she knew would come. The wind rattled the windows, heightening her anticipation, but there wasn't a sound from Manly. She looked hesitantly toward the edge of the bed. Either the fall had not awakened him or he was lying there, spread-eagled, with a concussion.

Slowly a tousled head of hair rose up over the edge of the mattress. It was followed by eyes that could have belonged to a polecat and the scowl of a hibernating bear who'd been awakened early. "Laura, I'm just goin' to ask you once," he said slowly. "Why'd you push me from the bed?"

Laura grinned sheepishly. "I was cold and wanted some of the quilt you were hogging, but when I pulled and pushed, you decided to roll over."

"You pushed me out of the bed! That's a heck of a way to wake someone up on a cold mornin'."

The windows rattled again. "Time to get up, anyway," she said, pulling the quilt completely around her and laying back down.

Manly's joints cracked as he stood up and stretched. The warmth of the bed was gone, and he shivered, feeling the chill in the air. He looked over at Laura. "I thought you said it was time to get up?"

She giggled under the covers. "Time for *you* to get up. Why don't you make me breakfast in bed?"

Manly took a step toward the window, but his nightshirt, caught on the knob of the nightstand, ripped loudly down the back.

Laura sat up quickly. "What happened?"

"Nothing. Just caught my shirt. Lay back down," he said, trying to unhook it.

Laura began giggling. Manly's behind was peeking out of his torn nightshirt. "I thought it was dawn, but the moon's still out," she laughed.

"What moon?" he asked, looking toward the frosted window.

Laura rolled about the bed, laughing. As a cold draft flew by his exposed backside, Manly blushed, pulling the nightshirt closed.

"You think that's funny, don't cha? Seein' me freeze my tail off while you're layin' there all snug and warm like a queen bee, hoggin' the quilt."

"You were the hog first," she said, wiping a tear of laughter from her eye.

Manly moved his finger across the window to clear a space. "Looks like we've had the first snow of the year."

"Snow?" she asked, sitting up. "How much did we get?"

" 'Bout three inches," Manly said, wiping a viewing space clear. *"Farmer's Almanac* said it'd come 'bout mid-November, and it's right on the button again. I don't see how they do it."

She snuggled under the covers. "Winter is a certainty. Spring and summer are only illusions."

Manly grabbed his pants from the back of the chair and quickly pulled them on. The dungarees felt cold on his legs. "Laura, where are my long johns?"

"In the top drawer, where they always are."

Manly took his pants off and stepped into his fire-engine-red long johns. Then he slipped back into his pants and pulled on a wool workshirt and a heavy sweater that Laura had knit for him.

Tapping on the window to clear some of the snow away, Manly turned to Laura. "Guess I've got my work cut out for me now."

"What's that?" Laura asked, standing up with the quilt wrapped around her. "The snow's not deep enough to worry about."

"First snow means butcherin' time," he said, pushing his foot into his left boot.

"Poor Bessie," Laura said. "I kind of like that old hog."

"Well, don't you worry," he said. "Once that old hog's gone, we got another to take its place."

"We do? Who?"

Manly pointed his finger at her. "You! You're always hoggin' the quilt. A man can't get a good sleep with you takin' the covers every night."

"Manly Wilder, you're the quilt hog." She oinked at him like a pig. He oinked back at her and stepped toward the door.

Laura called after him, " 'Bout that breakfast, Manly." She paused, giggling. "I'll have my eggs over easy, if you don't mind."

Manly threw her a look that said there'd be no breakfast in bed that day, and Laura shrugged. "Well, it was worth a shot, anyway," she said to herself as she dressed rapidly in the cold.

CHAPTER 2

TURTLEDOVE?

While Laura cooked up eggs and johnnycakes, Manly swept the snow from the front and back steps. Apple Hill Farm was covered with a glistening white blanket. The last geese of fall flew overhead in small V-formations, trying to catch their smarter cousins, who'd headed south during the peak of Indian summer.

Stomping the snow off his boots, Manly came into the kitchen and clapped his hands together for warmth. "Must be down near fifteen degrees," he said, warming himself next to the stove. "Had to use the axe to chop a hole in the horse's trough."

Laura was adding boiling water to a bowl of cornmeal. "Are you going to keep the livestock in the barns today?"

"I'll let the cows out mid-morning, when it's warmed up a bit." He watched her beating the cornmeal mixture smooth, licking his lips as she added butter, salt, eggs, and sugar. "Want me to help?" he asked, standing to her side, hoping she wouldn't see his fingers inching toward the warm sausage balls.

Laura slapped his hand with a spatula. "Keep your fingers

out of there. That's about the last of the sausage for you until you butcher old Bessie." The batter was smooth, so she carefully poured two big johnnycakes in the hot greased skillet. "Who's going to help you with the butchering this year?"

"I called Dr. George. He wants loin chops for helpin'."

"What about Maurice?"

Manly shrugged. "He always seems to know when it's butcherin' time." With a laugh he said, "Maurice always asks for the same thing."

"What's that?"

"Sow belly and ribs. Dr. George wants the good cuts, and Maurice always wants the poorer ones. Them two are as different as night and day."

Laura shook her head. "Did you tell Rev. Youngun to keep Sherry home at the first snow?"

"Oh, I knew I forgot somethin'! Would you call him?"

"I'll do it after breakfast." Laura paused, deep in thought. "You better keep an eye out for that little girl. She's been bringing an apple a day for the past week to Bessie. It'd break her heart to come over and find you butchering her animal friend."

Manly sighed. "I'll keep a lookout. If I see her comin', I'll call you to keep her away."

"Do you think it's right to fib to her about Bessie?" Laura asked.

Manly shook his head. "She's just too little to understand slaughterin' an animal for food—'specially one she's fallen in love with."

"Think she'll believe the story about sending Bessie to a hog farm upstate?"

"It's either that or tell the little girl that Bessie's gone to hog heaven when we offer her a ham sandwich." Manly chuckled to himself for a moment, then noticed Laura's frown. "I'm sorry. That wasn't very nice."

Laura went back to cooking. "Isn't it something the way little girls can fall in love with the strangest animals?"

Manly put his hands on Laura's waist and stole a quick kiss.

"Manly, I'm cooking breakfast. My hands are covered with batter and sausage grease. You think that's romantic?"

He reached out to grab her, and she slipped from his grasp again. "You're harder to catch than a greased piglet," he laughed, sneaking a sausage ball without her noticing.

Laura picked up the bowl of eggs. "Greased piglet? Manly Wilder, I may have a few extra pounds on me, but don't ever compare me to a greased piglet!"

"I like piglets, girl! They're cute, and they squeal a lot," he joked, winking. "Okay, okay," he laughed. "How about turtledove?"

"Turtledove? That's even worse! That's a big-breasted round bird that sits around all puffed out about itself."

Manly chuckled. "Two out of three ain't bad."

"Which two out of three?" she asked with a smile.

Stepping back and admiring her, Manly said, "Well, you sure have a nice figure, and you sure like to talk about yourself, don't cha?"

He ducked her playful slap and grabbed another sausage ball. In her rush, Laura picked up the pan without the pot holder and burned her fingers. "Ouch! See what you made me do?"

"Sorry, pigeon, I was . . ."

Laura spun on her heels to face him. "Pigeon? Now you're sayin' I'm like those dirty birds that hoot and poop all the time." With a mocking tone, she said, "How'd you like it if I called you 'Meadow Muffin' or 'Old Manure Spreader'?"

Manly laughed. "Land's sakes, girl, don't be so sensitive! We've been playin' like this for almost twenty years. You're thirty-eight years old. When you goin' to learn to take it?"

Laura turned around like a ballerina. "I know how to take it, silly. When are you going to realize that?" she asked. "And I may be thirty-eight years old but, old man, you're almost fifty."

"Old man, huh?" He pretended to walk hunched over, with an imaginary cane. In a squeaky voice, he wheezed, "Just too old to do anythin'—too old to catch my honeybee anymore."

With a quick grab, Manly wrapped his arms around Laura's waist, pulling her to him. He kissed her lips hard, and Laura's resistance folded as she melted into his arms. There was nothing else to say.

After breakfast, Manly helped dry the dishes as Laura washed.

"Manly, do you think Rose will make it home for Thanksgiving?"

He shook his head. "Her last letter said she was goin' to be here, but Thanksgivin's less than a week away. If it snows any harder, she might not be able to make it."

"Can't she take the train?" Laura asked.

"She's your daughter, and every bit as stubborn. I told her to take the train, but she said she had a ride with one of her high-school friends."

"I just hope the car makes it," Laura said, shaking her head. "These roads aren't very safe."

Manly stood behind his wife and smiled. Laura Ingalls Wilder, who'd been raised on the prairie, living in wagons and log cabins, was worried about the roads. A three-day ride in a car was nothing, compared to the many three-month wagon journeys she'd made with her pa, guided only by the sun and stars.

"She'll be all right," he said softly. "Rose will get home."

CHAPTER 3

HOG BUTCHERIN' TIME

Laura looked away from the bedroom window. Manly had Bessie by the ears, dragging her squealing from the pen. Dr. George had a rope around her neck and was pulling hard, but Bessie was fighting every step of the way. Farm animals always seemed to know when their time was up.

Dr. George was not used to farm ways, and found Bessie's end to be upsetting. "I can't imagine raisin' up a hog, givin' it a name, and then slittin' its throat."

It was all natural to Manly. "Doc, it's not like I took Bessie out dancin', or somethin'. You just give farm animals names. That's how it's done."

Dr. George tried to take his mind off Bessie. "You know that sailors in Europe believe you can't drown if you have a tattoo of a pig on one foot and a tattoo of a rooster on the other?"

Manly shook his head. "They'd be better off tattooing 'Save Me—I Can't Swim' on their foreheads. That kind of foolishness is what keeps the world off balance."

"Some people probably worship pigs somewhere," Dr.

George said. He chuckled. "In India they believe in reincarna-
tion."

"Re-in-what?" Manly asked.

"Life after death. You come back in another form. That's why
they don't kill their cows and eat 'em, like we do. They won't
kill bugs, either."

Manly snorted. "Believe what you want, George. Don't matter to me. But I don't believe in worshipin' my farm animals."

"I was just talkin', Manly, tryin' to get my mind off Bessie.
This slaughterin' is sure a messy business."

"Are you tellin' me you don't want loin chops for helpin'
me?"

"'Course I want loin chops. You think I'm doin' this for my
health? I'm just glad that I don't work in a packin' house." Dr.
George turned away, feeling dizzy.

Carefully Manly tapped him on the shoulder. "Feeling all
right, Doc?"

"I'll be okay. Just need some air," Dr. George answered,
turning around.

It took the doctor a few minutes to get back on his feet. Until
he was ready, Manly just kept on working. He got out the
chain, made sure the hoist was tight, and looped the chain
around the pig's carcass. When Dr. George was ready, they
lifted the carcass into a boiling tub of water. After a few minutes, they hoisted it back up and over onto the table. With their
sharp butcher knives, they scraped the hog's hair off, then
chained up the hind legs and hung it up over the guts tub.
With one swift stroke, Manly cut the hog open and cleaned the
hog.

While the hog carcass cooled off, Manly and Dr. George
sipped a cup of coffee. "What you goin' to do with that?" Dr.
George asked, looking at a bowl of fat.

"Laura's goin' to make lard from it."

"Lard? Why not just use butter?"

Manly laughed. "I told you, we use everything. We're going

to pack the big chunks of fat in salt and hang the hams that we don't cure in the icehouse until we eat them. Nuthin' goes to waste here."

"Hey, Manly," said a voice behind them, "what's for supper?" The two men turned to welcome Maurice Springer, Manly's neighbor and part-time laborer.

Though Maurice and Dr. George were friendly with each other, Manly had always felt they had a rivalry of some sort. He suspected that it was because Maurice was a farm laborer and Dr. George was a city boy, educated as a doctor. He wouldn't even have hazarded a guess that it was also because Maurice was dark-skinned and George's complexion was very light.

Manly stood up and inspected the carcass. "Maurice, I thought you were workin' in town today."

Maurice arched his eyebrows. "And not be part of the hog butcherin'? You know better! Dr. George, you bein' useful here, or just here for your chops?" Maurice slapped Dr. George on the back and rhymed, "You bowlegged, lazy, and almos' half crazy. You know that, Doc?"

Dr. George fumed. "I'm surprised you've lived this long, with that mouth of yours. If you had any brains, I'd be worried, but you don't." With that taunt, Dr. George spit between Maurice's feet.

The smile hardened on Maurice's face.

Manly finally spoke up. "What is it with you two?"

Maurice and Dr. George glared at each other for a moment. Then Maurice said, "This man thinks he's better'n me."

Dr. George snorted. "I do not."

"Oh yes, you do. Tell ol' Manly here how it is with our people."

Dr. George glared at Maurice. "You got something to say, you say it."

Maurice spoke to Manly, but he looked at Dr. George the whole time. "We got a saying among black folks:

If you white, you right,
If you yellow, you mellow,
If you brown, stick around,
But if you black, get back."

Maurice gestured toward Dr. George and his beige complexion. "This man here, he's mellow yellow, which is right under white is right." Maurice rolled up his sleeve to show his own ebony skin. "Me, I'm at the end of the line, where if you black, get back."

"Can't help what you can't help," Dr. George said.

"I never heard such a thing," said Manly, shaking his head. "You really think this way? How come you folks don't stick together?"

" 'Cause that's the way it is," Maurice said, looking a little sad. Suddenly he laughed and slapped the doctor on the back. "Hey, Doc, Manly's right. We got to stick together."

Dr. George looked none too interested.

Manly joined in. "Come on, Doc, Maurice is only kiddin' with you. Now cool it off, you two. We've got a hog to slaughter."

Dr. George shook his head, but he finally laughed. "Maurice, I'm sorry. I know you were just playin' with me. I've got a few things on my mind, that's all."

"Somethin' I can help you with, Doc?" Manly asked.

"It's such a terrible world to try and raise children in nowadays," Dr. George said.

Manly looked at Maurice with a question in his eyes. "I'm glad my Rose is about raised by now," Manly said, "but you've always said you were goin' to stay a bachelor all your life. You thinkin' 'bout gettin' married?"

Dr. George shook his head. "No, never wanted the responsibility. But now . . ." His voice trailed off as he looked down.

"Now what?" asked Maurice.

"My sister Janie, up in St. Louis, died of cancer."

"I'm sorry, Doc. I didn't know," Manly said.

"We weren't all that close, but she left everything to me in her will."

"Everything? Was she rich?" asked Maurice. "I always wanted to know a rich black doctor."

Dr. George let it pass. "She wasn't rich, but she didn't leave any debts, either. She'd been workin' as a seamstress since her husband got killed at the battle of San Juan Hill."

"That's good," said Maurice. "Nothin' worse than goin' to a funeral and gettin' a bill that you can't give back 'cause the deadbeat's skipped to the hereafter."

"What'd she leave you, then?" asked Manly.

"Did she have a car?" asked Maurice.

"No, she never owned a car. She just worked hard at gettin' by."

"Well, what did she leave you then?" Maurice asked again.

"C.E.," Dr. George said, without explaining.

"C.E.?" questioned Maurice. "What's a C.E.?"

Manly and Maurice watched the doctor's face, waiting for an answer. He spoke softly. "C.E. stands for Cubby Elliott, my eight-year-old nephew. She left me a letter sayin' she wants me to raise him."

"That's wonderful!" Maurice shouted. "You're an instant daddy!"

Manly said quietly, "That's why you were sayin' this is a bad world to bring up children in."

"Yeah," said Dr. George. "I never thought 'bout it until I got the letter. Now I look around and see nothin' but trouble, hate, and hard times all around."

"It's always been that way, Dr. George. Always will be," Maurice said.

"We all overlook what we don't have to see," said Manly. "When's Cubby comin'?"

Dr. George looked at his watch. "Be here on the noon train tomorrow."

"What's he look like?" Maurice asked. "How you goin' to recognize him?"

"I haven't seen him in several years," he said, pulling out a picture. "This was with the letter."

Maurice took the picture and whistled. "He's a handsome boy. He sure is." He paused for a moment, holding the picture up against Dr. George's face. "Why, he must be from the African side of your family, 'cause he's black as midnight and you're as light as you can be."

"Maurice, will you let up?" Dr. George snapped. He turned to Manly. "What'll I do? What am I going to do with an eight-year-old?"

"You'll do all right," Manly said. "Just bring him around and let Laura feed him."

"Eulla Mae will fatten him up," Maurice said proudly.

Dr. George just shook his head. "I've delivered most every baby in town, sewed up cuts and scratches, and looked down the throats of everyone else, including you two, but . . ."

"But what?" asked Maurice.

"But I ain't never bought a child clothes, worried about school, or had to tuck a little boy in at night. I'm a bachelor, not a daddy."

Manly sighed. "No doubt about it, Dr. George, Cubby's goin' to change your life."

"I know, I know," Dr. George lamented, slowly shaking his head.

Maurice chuckled. "Now all you got to do is marry a woman who can cook and hug, and you'll be happy for the rest of your life."

Winking at Manly, Maurice walked around the gutted pig hanging between them and then turned to Dr. George. "Now, I wonder where we can find you a *big* woman. One with the shape of old Bessie, here," he said, slapping the carcass. "I need to introduce you to my wife's sister, Polly."

"Maurice, I never said I liked big women."

"I tell you, ain't nothin' better to keep you warm on a cold Missouri night than a chubby, smilin' wife. You'd freeze to death, married to a skinny woman in Missouri!"

The three men laughed as the wind swung Bessie's carcass.

Up on the hill, little fingers spread the leaves apart and gasped. "Bessie. My poor Bessie," a small voice moaned as an apple rolled down the icy slope.

CHAPTER 4

AN APPLE FOR BESSIE

Sherry Youngun had skipped and sung Christmas songs along the path from her house to Apple Hill Farm. For the past three weeks she had brought an apple to Bessie every day.

Her love for Bessie began one day when she went with her father to visit the Wilders. While her father, Rev. Youngun, talked of the church's financial needs, Sherry took the opportunity to explore the barn and play with the cats.

But it was Bessie the hog she'd fallen in love with. There was just something about the big pink hog that attracted her. Though she could have picked a lamb, goat, cat, cow, or dog, Bessie was the lucky one Sherry had given her heart to.

A few weeks ago, Manly had found Sherry in the barn, petting Bessie. He had an apple in his hand and was about to take a bite. Instead, he held it out for Sherry to take. "Feed it to her, Sherry. Bessie loves red apples. Helps her stay pretty and pink."

"Are you sure, Mr. Wilder? Will she bite my hand?" Sherry asked.

"Go on, Sherry, take it. She won't bite you. Bessie loves pretty little girls who feed her apples."

Sherry hesitantly held the apple in front of Bessie, but she stepped back when the pig squealed in anticipation of the treat. She tossed the apple into Bessie's mouth, then laughed and clapped as the big pink pig devoured it. She was so delighted at the sounds that Bessie made that she came back every day with an apple.

Bessie would grunt and squeal as the hands of the five-year-old girl moved the apple back and forth. "All right, Bessie," she'd finally say, "here's your apple." Bessie would take the apple off the fence and devour it greedily.

At school she drew pictures of the pig and made up a song about her. Sherry even included Bessie in the imaginary doll games that she played in her closet. "Pa," Sherry had asked one evening when he was tucking her into bed, "is it all right to ask God to bless Bessie the pig?"

Rev. Youngun looked down at his button-cute daughter. "Why, sure it is. God made all the people and all the animals."

Seven-year-old brother Terry piped up from the next bedroom, "Oink, oink, oink! Sherry loves a p-i-g!"

"Don't let him bother you," her father said. "It's all right to love an animal."

Terry came into the doorway, his mop of auburn hair all astray. "Why don't you tell her that they'll soon be makin' bacon from Bessie?"

"Will not, will not!" Sherry screamed.

"Roses are red, rain is water, winter's arrived, it's time to slaughter!" His laughter echoed throughout the house. Terry made a face and pretended to slit his throat with his finger.

Sherry stuck her tongue out, and Terry ran from the doorway. "That wasn't nice," Sherry said to her father.

"No, it wasn't. I guess Terry doesn't understand what Bessie means to you."

Terry knocked on the wall. "Hey, Sherry, you know what P-I-G stands for?"

"What?" she reluctantly asked back.

"P-I-G stands for Pig Is Good eatin'."

"He's a red-haired idiot," Sherry said to her father.

"That's not nice. Don't say that about your brother," Rev. Youngun said, thinking of the names *he* had for his squirrel-headed, auburn-haired son.

"Did Ma love animals?" Sherry asked. She was always asking questions about her mother, who'd died of the fever.

"Your mother had a big heart. She was kind to animals, just like you are."

"Can we buy Bessie from the Wilders and bring her home to live with us?" she asked hopefully. "I could keep her in the kitchen and feed her from my plate."

"We'll see," her father said. "We'll see."

"I could make her a big, pink dress and bonnet and . . ."

"Time to sleep, young lady." He tucked Sherry in, putting out the lamp by the bed.

As Rev. Youngun walked down the stairs, Terry let out a loud "Souieeeeee, souieeeeeee."

"Stop it, Terry!" Rev. Youngun shouted out. "You're askin' for a spankin'!"

As the house quieted down, Rev. Youngun sat in the dark in his reading chair. With butchering time coming up, he was concerned about Sherry's attachment to Bessie. He'd already mentioned it to Laura, who was aware of the looming problem. They knew how upset Sherry would be if she found out that Bessie was going to be slaughtered and happily eaten by everyone, including Sherry.

So Rev. Youngun and Laura had agreed to a little white lie. They were going to tell Sherry that Bessie had been sent to a happy pig farm and would certainly miss her little friend.

Rev. Youngun was as uncomfortable as Laura was, telling Sherry the fib. Call it a white lie, call it a bold-faced lie—they both knew that adults excuse fibs to children as being in the child's best interest.

Deep in his heart, Rev. Youngun knew that the fib was really in *his* best interest. As parents everywhere believed, some things are just too hard to explain to a child. So they put them off until they are absolutely forced to discuss them.

The problem was that Laura had forgotten to call Rev. Youngun that morning, to tell him it was slaughtering time. So Sherry took an apple from the bin in the basement and walked through the snow to the Wilders', as if everything were fine.

Sherry had gone over the trail as happy as a lark, singing her version of "Jingle Bells": "Jingle Bells, jingle bells, jingle all the weight, Oh what fun it is to ride, in a one-horse open sled."

A hoot owl interrupted her song. She made a snowball and tossed it at the snowy owl on the branch, but it fell far short.

She bounced along, thinking about what she'd get Bessie for Christmas. Maybe that bonnet she'd dreamed about, or a pretty leather collar. She wondered if Pa would mind if she made a soft rag bed at the foot of her own bed for Bessie. *Too cold for Bessie to sleep outside,* she thought.

The last part of the journey was always the happiest, because she'd call out Bessie's name and hear her squeal back a greeting. She looked down from the top of the hill toward her pen. "Bessie, Bessie, here comes Momma Sherry." But Bessie didn't come out from her stall. *That's not like Bessie,* Sherry thought to herself.

She skipped along the path and noticed the smoke and steam rising through the trees. Parting the leaves with her little fingers, she stopped and paled, her face stark white and her body trembling.

The apple rolled from her hand, red against the white snow, like the blood below Bessie's swinging, gutted carcass. "Bessie, Bessie," she moaned, as a single tear streaked down her cheek.

Down below her, standing next to the twisting carcass, the three men stopped their laughing and looked up. A long, piercing wail of sorrow bounced across the trees and ridges.

"Oh, no!" Manly moaned, shaking his head. He saw Laura

come out on the back porch and shouted at her, "Didn't you tell Rev. Youngun to keep that girl home?"

"Oh, Lord," Laura said, coming down the back stairs. "I forgot. That poor child."

While the other two men stood there, Maurice started up the hill. "Baby, baby, it'll be all right."

Dr. George was without a clue. "What's this all about?"

Manly shook his head in dismay. "Rev. Youngun's daughter fell in love with Bessie," he said, pointing to the gutted pig. "Laura was supposed to call her daddy to keep her home on butcherin' day."

Up on the hill, Maurice had Sherry in his arms, hugging her tightly. He loved that little girl as if she were his own. "Baby, baby, it'll be all right. You're with Maurice now. Bessie's in heaven, baby. She's in heaven now."

"They killed her," she moaned. "Pa was going to buy her for me."

"Bessie was a farm animal, Sherry. Pigs are raised for food."

"Not Bessie! She was my friend," she whimpered.

Maurice kissed her forehead. "Girl, it's hard to understand."

"Bessie was special," she sobbed, sinking her face into Maurice's chest.

"Everything living is special. It all has a special place and purpose," whispered Maurice. He looked down and saw her eyes staring at the hanging hog. Shielding them with his hand, he spun around. Laura was standing there.

"What'd you tell her?" Laura whispered.

"Somebody's got to begin tellin' this girl the truth!" he said. "Life's hard enough without takin' on hurts you don't need to carry."

CHAPTER 5

TEDDY ROOSEVELT

S herry lay still in Maurice's arms all the way home. Laura tried to keep up with them, but Maurice's determined step was too much for her, so she walked behind in silence. Rev. Youngun saw them coming and knew without asking what had happened.

"Today was the day for Bessie, wasn't it?" he asked.

Maurice nodded. "What she saw was bad. Real bad."

Laura shook her head. "I should have called. I should . . ."

Rev. Youngun held up his hand. "Just an accident, Laura. Just one of those hard things that happen in life." He took his daughter from Maurice's arms and smoothed back her hair. "I'll put her to bed. She needs rest."

Rev. Youngun carried Sherry up the stairs and put her to bed. He kissed her forehead and pulled the blanket up. Tears were running down her cheeks, but she wasn't saying anything. "I'm so sorry about Bessie," he whispered. "I'm so sorry."

Sherry looked up. "They killed her, Pa. They slit her throat and pulled her insides out. Why, Pa? Why?"

"There are some things that are just hard to understand, Sherry."

Her lips were quivering. "Why didn't *they* understand I loved her?"

Before he could answer, she buried her face in the pillow. He didn't know what to say and thought it best to leave her alone for a while, so he trudged downstairs, deep in thought, and made coffee. While it brewed, he, Maurice, and Laura sat in the kitchen, somberly talking about how hard it is to grow up.

"I've got another problem comin' up," Rev. Youngun said.

"What's that?" Maurice asked.

"Teddy Roosevelt," Rev. Youngun said, shaking his head.

"The president? What problem you got with President Roosevelt?" Maurice exclaimed.

"Not the president. I'm talkin' about the turkey." Rev. Youngun sighed. "Bessie was bad enough, but one of the parishioners gave us a tom turkey this spring. We've been feedin' and fattin' him up for Thanksgiving."

A turkey gobbled outside, and Laura smiled.

"The kids have named him Teddy Roosevelt. T.R. for short. After what just happened to Sherry and her pig, how am I goin' to explain killin' T.R. and eatin' him?"

The turkey gobbled again, and Rev. Youngun looked out the window. The three adults began laughing as they watched Larry and Terry march around like soldiers, leading the reluctant turkey on a leash.

"It's a strange world where we have some animals for pets and others for food," Laura said, after the laughter had subsided.

"Why'd you name that bird Teddy Roosevelt? Don't you like the president?" Maurice asked.

Rev. Youngun laughed. "I didn't name him. Sherry did. When we were given the bird, she'd just seen a picture of the president speaking in St. Louis. She thought the gobble-bag hanging from the bird's neck looked like the big moustache on the president's face." Rev. Youngun paused for a moment, then said with a grin, "Maybe that's why I didn't vote for him."

"Maybe I should have voted instead of goin' fishin'," Maurice said sheepishly.

Laura said, with a frosty tone, "At least you both were able to vote. Women aren't considered smart enough to vote in this country." Her comment hung in the air. Neither man dared to look her in the face for a moment.

Finally Maurice spoke up. "Well, heck. If this is gonna to be a women-votin' meetin', I'll just shut my mouth. My Eulla Mae gets so worked up that once she chased me out of the kitchen with a rolling pin."

The way he said it made Laura laugh. Maurice continued. "If it was up to me, I'd have women run the country. They durn sure run everything now, so why kid ourselves? Why, at my house I can't even get a nickel for a cold soda without first goin' through a grillin' from Eulla Mae. Give women the vote, I say. It'll get 'em off their husbands' backs."

"I'll vote for that," Rev. Youngun laughed.

"You can vote for that, but you still got a problem with Teddy Roosevelt out there," Maurice said, pointing to the two boys leading the turkey around the yard.

"What am I goin' to do? They'll be expectin' a turkey dinner at Thanksgiving."

"Have a ham instead," Maurice said, without thinking. "Oh, sorry. Guess Sherry would be of no mind to eat ham after seein' Bessie and all."

"Just tell them the truth," Laura said.

"Okay," Rev. Youngun said, "why don't you march out there and tell them to cut Teddy Roosevelt's head off for Thanksgiving dinner?"

"It's either that or concoct another fib, which we haven't been too good at," Laura said quietly.

Maurice scratched his head. "I got it!" They both looked at him. He grinned broadly.

"Well?" Rev. Youngun asked, "what's the answer?"

"Guess," Maurice laughed. He began strutting around the room, gobbling, spreading his arms over his head. Laura and Rev. Youngun were mystified. "Come on, guess," Maurice laughed, gobbling and spreading his arms. "What do I look like?"

"A dummy," chuckled Rev. Youngun.

Maurice shook his head. "Laura, you know the answer?"

Laura smiled, "You look like a big turkey, waving your arms overhead, praying for Thanksgiving to be cancelled."

"That's good. That's a good one," Maurice laughed. "I got the answer to your problems, Rev. Youngun."

"Pray, please tell me," Rev. Youngun said.

"A turkey tree," Maurice said, grinning.

"A what?" Laura exclaimed.

"A turkey tree. I'll show your kids where to find the turkey tree."

"I've never heard of such a thing," Laura said. "Are you pulling our leg?"

"No, ma'am! I know where there's a secret turkey tree."

"How's this goin' to help Teddy Roosevelt?" Rev. Youngun asked.

With a big smile, Maurice began. "You have to tell 'em where meat comes from and why we eat animals. That can't be avoided if you live around farms." He sipped his coffee, then winked. "But if they can catch another turkey at the turkey tree, then old Teddy Roosevelt can keep his head for another year."

Maurice was interrupted by a knock on the door. "Pa," asked Terry, "can you give us a piece of bread to feed Teddy Roosevelt? He's starvin!"

Rev. Youngun looked at Laura and Maurice. "Where is this turkey tree, Maurice?"

"Not too far," Maurice said, chuckling to himself as Terry took the bread and fed it to the turkey.

Larry stuck his head through the doorway. "Pa, do you have some old gloves?"

He looked at his son's gloved hands. "Who needs them?"

Larry grinned. "Teddy Roosevelt," he said, as if it were obvious to the world. "I'm worried that his feet will get cold during our march."

"His feet will be all right," Rev. Youngun said. "Now you boys go out and play."

Maurice stood up as the Rev. Youngun sat back down. "Hope little Sherry gets to feelin' better soon," he said, taking his empty coffee cup and placing it next to the sink. "I got to be goin'. Thank you for the coffee."

"Maurice, are you pulling a trick on us with this so-called turkey tree?" Laura asked.

"No." Maurice looked at Rev. Youngun. "If you tell them 'bout eatin' meat, I'll show 'em where to find the turkey tree in a few days." He stepped out the door, then quickly stuck his head back inside, "Rev. Youngun?"

"Yes?"

"Do me one favor, will ya?" Maurice said, winking at Laura.

"Sure. What is it?" Rev. Youngun asked.

Maurice smiled, then bumped his head on the doorjamb. "Dangit, that hurts!" From under the porch steps came a growl, and Dangit the dog, the Younguns' mutt, came rushing out, grabbing onto Maurice's pants' legs. "Get that dog off me!" he screamed.

Larry came up and pulled the dog off. "Sorry, Mr. Springer. Dangit just don't like people to misuse his name."

Maurice grumbled, rubbing his ankle. "Glad you didn't name that darn dog 'outhouse' or we'd all be in trouble."

Laura was laughing too hard to speak. Finally Rev. Youngun was able to wipe a tear of laughter from his eye and ask, "What's the favor, Maurice?"

"Oh, I was goin' to ask you to not let Sherry go namin' all

my look-alike rabbits Peter. I'd be starvin' to death without my rabbit hutch, come Easter time."

"I'll tell them about why we eat meat, if you show them the turkey tree," Rev. Youngun agreed.

"My job's easier than yours," Maurice said over his shoulder. Within moments he was out of sight along the path.

Larry knocked on the door. "Pa, Crab Apple the mule wants an apple, and Teddy Roosevelt wants another piece of bread." He stood there with his hat off.

"Anything else?" Rev. Youngun asked.

"Can Dangit have a meatball from the icebox?"

Laura watched Larry jump off the edge of the porch with the animal treats clutched in his hand. She turned to Rev. Youngun. "I'm just thankful your kids weren't running Noah's Ark. They'd have let every single animal alive on board, and the boat would have sunk."

Rev. Youngun smiled and shook his head. "Kids have their own world. That's why they're kids."

"Thanks for the coffee," she said, and headed home.

Upstairs, Sherry put her drawing of Bessie under her pillow and prayed. "God, please bring Bessie back to me."

CHAPTER 6

CUBBY ELLIOTT

Dr. George didn't even see the deep pothole that nearly knocked his car off the road. He waved to one of the church ladies and looked at his watch. Eleven forty-five. Cubby's train was due at noon.

He pulled behind the station and waited for the approaching whistle. How quickly time had passed since he'd accepted the job in Mansfield. Memories flooded back upon him. It'd been fifteen years since he'd come to town on the noon train from St. Louis, and now he was waiting at the same station for the same train to change his life a second time.

He'd never asked to take on the responsibility of his late sister's eight-year-old son, but what was he to do? Leave the boy with the church in St. Louis? *You can't hide from responsibility without scarring your soul,* he remembered his mother saying.

Dr. George had seen too many people close their eyes to the need around them, and so he had always tried to conduct his practice by the Golden Rule. In a world where color made a big difference in how you were treated, he still tried to treat others as he wanted to be treated. But being a successful black man in America was difficult, at best.

You intimidate them, his mother told him. *They expect you to be ignorant,* she said on his first day of medical school. *Your education will always set you apart from both blacks and whites.*

Then there was the added burden of being light-skinned. His mother had been a true albino, with pale eyes and ghost-white hair, but his father had been very dark. Dr. George was lighter than most of the blacks around him. His skin was a light tan shade. He'd listened often enough to his mother about the hurts of the world that awaited him, but even her warning and love could not keep all the hurt away. He always thought that, by working harder and getting better grades than everyone else, he would finally get respect. He had been wrong.

If not for his mother, he probably would have dropped out of medical school. The white students from the wealthy homes and East Coast schools treated him as if he had a disease. He was the brunt of cruel jokes and hoaxes. None of the white teachers would be his mentor.

When he graduated, the white boys got offers from the big-city hospitals. He waited in vain for the mailman to bring him an answer to all the letters he'd sent out, looking for work. The big-city hospital applications always required a picture, and though he was light-skinned, his race was still obvious. He dreaded the question found on every job application:

Race? White_____Other_____
If other, please describe:

What was he to put down? *Other* than being a smart, light-skinned black doctor, I'm a human being.

At the same time, Mansfield, Missouri, was without a doctor. Andrew Jackson Summers, editor of the *Mansfield Monitor,* had written the medical school to ask if any of the new doctors would move to Mansfield. He described the country, the people, and everything else that would make up for the probability of getting paid in friendship, chickens, and very little money. An announcement had been posted at the school, and in desperation Dr. George had answered it, not expecting a reply.

Then came the call from Summers. Dr. George took the phone call on the hall telephone. "This is George. Can I help you?"

"I hope so," came a garbled voice from the phone, "but I thought you were *Dr.* George." It was the voice of a white man, with the twang of a Southern accent.

Looking at the phone, Dr. George marveled at how easy conversation was between whites and blacks when they couldn't see each other.

"This is Dr. George. Who am I speaking with?"

"This is Andrew Jackson Summers, editor of the *Mansfield Monitor.* You answered my ad for a small-town doctor."

Dr. George instantly became alert. "Where's Mansfield? What state is it in?"

"It's in the nice part of the same state you're standin' in. About an hour east of Springfield. When can you be here?"

"Is there an emergency?" Dr. George asked.

"Town can't grow without a doctor. There's babies comin' and old people who need doctorin'. We can offer you a small house, horse and buggy, and enough apples, potatoes, and chickens to feed you for the first year."

Dr. George's heart ached. It was obvious that the man didn't know he was black. "Did you get my picture?" he asked quietly.

"Yeah," said Summers, "but we're not runnin' a beauty contest here, so you'll do."

"Did you notice that I'm black?" Dr. George said, shaking with nervousness.

"Let me look again," Summers said. "Yup, you're black, all right. Blacks 'round here might call you high-yellow, but that hair's a dead giveaway." His last words were almost drowned out by static.

"Does that bother you?" Dr. George asked, hoping Summers would hear him.

"Dr. George," Summers said as the line cleared up, "I don't care if you're bald and blue. We need a doctor, and you're lookin' for a job." He paused, and as he tried to speak again, the phone line went garbled, then cleared up. ". . . I asked you, when can you be here? Mrs. Johnson's baby's due any day now."

Dr. George laughed and let out a long sigh of relief. "You got a train station in Mansfield?"

It was Summers's turn to laugh. "Doc, we got a train depot, the blacksmith almost killed himself in his homemade airplane, and we've got six motor cars fouling up the air. Other than that, you'll like it here."

"I'll have to check the train schedule," Dr. George said.

Summers chuckled. "I've already checked it for you. The St. Louis to Mansfield train leaves tomorrow mornin' at six A.M. It'll be here at noon. There'll be a ticket at the station waitin' for you, and I'll pick you up when you get here."

Dr. George smiled. "How will I recognize you?"

"I'll be the only white man at the station callin' you Doctor. Be on that train, Doc. We need you." Summers clicked off the line and thus changed Dr. George's life forever.

That was fifteen years ago, and now another scared black person was coming on the train, another person whose life was about to change. C.E. was coming—Cubby Elliott. The boy was coming to change his life, and it worried Dr. George no end.

The approaching whistle of the train brought him back around to the present. He hurried up to the arrival platform. People were scurrying back and forth. Porters carried bags, the train master was selling tickets, and nervous passengers said good-bye to loved ones.

He wondered about the legacy his mother had left him, a

legacy that he'd never really thought about. One thing she'd left him was evident in the voice he heard from behind him. He was now a respected doctor. "Hi, Dr. George," said Sheriff Peterson. "Thanks for lookin' in on my mother the other day."

Dr. George tipped his hat. "She'll be fine. Just needs someone to talk to every now and then. Make time for her, okay?"

Another legacy his mother left him came from across the platform: friendship. Stephen Scales, the telegraph operator, shouted, "Doc, you still plannin' to go fishin' with me tomorrow?"

"Sorry, Stephen, I can't. Got a relative comin' in on the noon train." Dr. George waved good-bye to Scales and realized that he'd spoken as if Cubby Elliott was coming for just a short visit.

The train pulled into the station. The smoke from the engine momentarily enveloped the platform, and when it cleared, a small black boy was standing in front of him. "Are you my uncle?" said the boy, who was wearing a Sunday suit and carrying a cloth suitcase.

Dr. George reached out and shook his hand. "Cubby?"

"I'm Cubby Elliott," he said, shaking the doctor's hand. "Should I call you Doctor, Uncle, or Daddy?"

Dr. George stiffened, thinking his bachelor ways were about to face a severe adjustment. "You can call me Uncle or Doc," Dr. George said, then realized that his mother had also left him a sense of responsibility.

"How about Peepaw?" Cubby said suddenly. "Momma said they used to call you that. That some kind of Indian name or something?"

Dr. George shook his head, remembering how that name got started when his poppa used to change his diapers. No, this would not do! "Son, you ever call me that 'round here, and you and I'll have a harsh man-to-man talk." He straightened his coat and said, with a certain amount of pride, "I'm the doctor of this town. People respect me and call me Dr. George."

Cubby frowned. "Can I call you Pops?"

"Pop or Pops will do," Dr. George said, picking up the boy's suitcase.

He took Cubby by the hand and walked to his Rambler automobile, parked outside the small station. When Cubby saw it, he stood back.

"Mama said you were rich, but woo-ee! I never saw a black man drivin' a car like this!"

Dr. George tossed the bag into the backseat. "Cubby, the only difference between rich and poor is hard work and education."

"I never knew a rich black man." Cubby ran his hand over the car's fender.

Dr. George lifted Cubby up. "See that poor black farmer over there?" he said, pointing to the old black man in the rickety wagon. Cubby nodded. "And you see that poor white man over there?" he said, pointing to a stooped-over Okie in a tattered coat. Cubby nodded again. Dr. George put him down.

He looked Cubby in the face. "Well, don't you ever forget that the difference between them and me and them and you is this much," Dr. George said, holding up his thumb and forefinger, just a hair apart. He looked at Cubby sternly. "I'm not rich, but I'm a smart, hard-working doctor who has respect. Don't be thinkin' all blacks got to be poor."

Cubby climbed into the front seat, trying to understand what he'd just heard. "Then you must be the smartest, hardest-workin' black man in Missouri, to have a car like this," he said, admiring the controls.

Dr. George rolled his eyes in exasperation. He started up the engine, backed up, then pulled slowly forward. Cubby put his hands over his eyes. "What's wrong?" asked Dr. George.

"I ain't never ridden in a car before."

Dr. George patted the boy on the back. "There's a lot of things you'll be discoverin' with me." *And I'll be discoverin' things being with you,* he thought.

Over the noise of the engine, Dr. George asked, "Anybody

ever told you about the great civilizations that existed in Africa while white men were huddled in caves in France? About the black pharaohs who built pyramids white men can't build today?"

"No," said Cubby, shaking his head.

"Anybody ever tell you about George Washington Carver?" Dr. George asked.

"Never heard of him," Cubby said, covering his eyes as they went around a curve.

Dr. George shook his head and decided to change the subject. "Anybody ever tell you about Santa Claus?"

Cubby nodded yes. "But I don't believe in Santa." He put his head down.

"Don't believe in Santa?" Dr. George exclaimed. "Christmas is almost here, so you'd better decide if you want Santa to come or not."

"Santa could never bring what I want."

"What you want? A new bike?" Dr. George said, searching for words to stop the boy from crying.

"All I'd want for Christmas . . . all I'd ever want . . . is to have my momma back."

Dr. George reached over and pulled the crying boy against him. "I miss my momma, too, Cubby. Mommas are the greatest ladies in every boy's life. Your momma gave you life and breathed her best into you, every day she was alive."

Dr. George thought about his own mother. His momma had been his best buddy, always there when he needed to talk, the only one he was comfortable talking about things with.

She'd helped him understand about tenderness, about girls, about being his own person. He could remember asking his mother how she knew so much about teenage girls, and she'd just whispered, " 'Cause I was one, honey."

Cubby interrupted his thoughts. "I want her back, Pe . . . Pops. I want her back."

"Sayin' good-bye to your momma is the hardest good-bye of all. Your momma's in a better place."

"She is?" Cubby said, wiping his tears on his sleeve.

"Sure is! But she wants you to do one thing for me."

"What's that?" Cubby asked.

"She wants you to never, I mean *never,* call me Peepaw again!"

Cubby broke up laughing and hugged his new Pops.

CHAPTER 7

HANDS OFF

The night brought another two feet of snow, and the temperature dropped to zero. With a cold winter ahead, people were covering drafty windows and laying down their winter rugs.

When word reached Mansfield that the road to Springfield had been blocked by snowdrifts, people grumbled, but they didn't panic. There was still the back road down toward Arkansas, and the rails were still open for the supply trains.

The merchants didn't jack up the prices on goods, because they were all expecting a full shipment by Thanksgiving, which was right around the corner. The butcher had a supply of turkeys ready to be killed and had put a smoker out back to smoke some of the birds.

Rev. Youngun had a hard time doing his ministering, because it was hard to get through in his wagon. Manly lent him a sleigh, so he could get back into the hills to help the infirm.

Sheriff Peterson was working double shifts. He and the farmers from the Congregational church were delivering food and chopping firewood for the elderly.

Dr. George was busy getting used to Cubby Elliott. He'd converted his big clothes closet into a little bedroom and made a bed from an old wagon seat he'd taken in trade for setting a broken arm. It was actually quite cozy, and Cubby seemed to like being close to his new Pops.

People still needed Dr. George's services, and he was embarrassed when all his lady friends volunteered to come over and babysit. Dr. George knew they were thinking he was in quick need of a wife, so he took the boy on some of his rounds to avoid the problem.

Cubby had never been around farms, and he loved the animals. But the snow kept coming, and the Rambler just wouldn't start up every time he needed it, so Dr. George borrowed a sleigh from the livery and took Cubby on his first sleigh ride.

Most of his patients and look-in-ons were doing fine, but Dr. George was very worried about a hill woman named Martha Helling. She was eight months pregnant, but from the pains she was experiencing, she could deliver at any time. Martha was thirty-eight-years-old and pregnant for the first time. It started out as a happy occasion, because she had thought she would never have a child, but as she neared full term, false-labor pains had started and never seemed to let up.

On every visit to the Hellings' small cabin, Dr. George sat very formally next to his bedridden patient. "Martha, you're almost forty years old. This pregnancy could kill you, if you're not careful."

"I know, Dr. George. I know," she said, looking toward Jacob Helling.

"She's been takin' her aspirin powder when she gets feverish," Jacob grumbled. "She'll be all right." He saw Dr. George fiddle around the edge of the bed and peered over his shoulder. "You finished yet?"

"He just got here, Jacob," his wife said. "Doctor, sometimes my head feels like it's burnin' up."

Jacob shook his head. "I keep tellin' her the aspirin powder is all she needs."

Dr. George looked at Jacob. "Just keep cold cloths on her forehead. That's a better way to keep the fever down at this stage of pregnancy."

It took him a moment to soak another cloth, which he carefully handed to Martha. "Are you eating well?" he asked, looking at her sternly.

"I'm cravin' bacon and salt pork," she smiled. "Can't seem to get 'nough of it."

Dr. George laughed. "Cravin' salt is Mother Nature's way of tellin' you that you're not gettin' enough salt with your meals."

"Land's sakes!" she exclaimed. "I thought I was goin' bacon crazy!" she laughed.

Dr. George smiled. "No, your body needs salt, and the unborn baby floats in a sac of salty fluid. Your baby is takin' salt from your system, so that's why you're cravin' salty foods."

She smiled, then winced from a pain. "It hurts, Doc."

Dr. George leaned forward but quickly sat back when Jacob came and stood beside the bed. "Are you all right?" he asked with a worried look on his face.

Martha winced, then gave a weak smile. "Doc, think maybe I ate too much of that lamb last night," she said, wincing again.

Dr. George looked at her husband. "Jacob, you make sure that you cook her meat until it's well-done. She can catch a disease called toxoplasmosis, which is as dangerous as German measles. Might retard the baby."

"You finished now?" Jacob asked curtly.

There was a limit to what Dr. George could do, because Jacob Helling didn't want a black man touching his wife. Dr. George remembered the last time he ran into this kind of prejudice. Back when he was studying to become a doctor, he practiced medicine in free health clinics. Every now and then, white patients didn't want Dr. George touching them because of his race. It didn't matter how sick those people were. And the doctoring was even free. This amazed Dr. George then, and it still did.

Now he was faced with Jacob Helling, whose wife could easily die without Dr. George's help. *And it would be her old man's racism that would kill her,* he thought. But all he could do was sit by Martha's bed, patiently talking with her, explaining the things she should do and signs she should look for. Jacob would stand behind him like a hawk, only agreeing to let a black man this close to his wife because there wasn't any other doctor around.

If Dr. George couldn't examine her, he couldn't tell how far along she was or know when she was ready to give birth. It was like trying to diagnose someone by telephone; it never worked. But no matter how hard he tried to explain to her husband, Jacob still figured he and Martha could deliver the baby themselves.

The baby was off to the side inside its mother and appeared to be in a cramped position. Although babies are usually born head first, sometimes they are born breech, or bottom first. It looked to Dr. George as if this might be a breech birth. He knew that lots of dangerous things could happen if Martha Helling was to go through a breech birth without his help. Both the mother and the baby could die.

To the baby floating inside the womb, color meant nothing. As the little heart thumped into the stethoscope, Dr. George looked at Jacob Helling. "For the love of God, man, think about your wife and baby. Yes, I'm a black man, but I'm a *doctor.* I'm not going to hurt your wife."

Jacob Helling, son of a Southern sharecropper, shook his head. "Just keep your hands off my wife. This be her idea, not mine."

Dr. George shook his head, packing up his bag. "You ever met Curly Joe Thomas, the undertaker's assistant?"

"Seen him around," said Jacob. "Why you askin'?"

"Well, sir, maybe you haven't noticed, but Curly Joe is a

black man." Dr. George paused, looking Jacob Helling directly in the eye. "And if you don't let me deliver your baby, his black hands just might put your wife in the coffin."

Dr. George left the small hill cabin without saying another word. Martha Helling pleaded with her husband to reconsider, but Jacob just eyed Dr. George through the window and shook his head.

Down the hill, Dr. George pulled the sleigh to a halt at the crossroads. He hadn't spoken a word to Cubby since leaving the house. Now Cubby asked quietly, "How'd it go back there? When you gonna deliver her baby?"

"It's out of my hands now, son. I've done about all I can."

"Aren't you a doctor?" Cubby asked, not understanding.

"I want to be, but that man won't let me help." Dr. George cracked the reins and ducked a branch.

"I don't understand," Cubby said, a perplexed look on his face.

"I don't either, son. I don't either."

For the rest of the trip back to town, they rode in silence through the snowy hillsides. That evening, as Cubby lay in his wagon-seat bed, Dr. George sat beside him, deep in thought. The emotions running through his head were miles and years away.

Looking at Cubby was like looking through a window to the past. He could remember his mother sitting beside him each night, softly talking about events of the day or whatever was on his mind.

Dr. George smiled to himself, remembering those bedtimes. His little conscience would twist and turn if something was bothering him. His mother would sit patiently, waiting for him to speak in his own time. *I could never go to sleep until I'd told Mother everything,* he remembered.

"Pops, do you say prayers when you go to sleep?" Cubby asked.

"Cubby, when I was your age, I said my prayers every night

with my. . . ." He hesitated, not wanting to bring up Cubby's recent hurt.

"With your mother. It's all right, Pops. My momma said the Lord's Prayer every night with me." Scratching his leg, then his arm, he asked, "Did you say the Lord's Prayer with your momma?"

"My mother and I had a special prayer that we made up together. We said it every night before I went to sleep."

"Would you teach it to me?" Cubby asked eagerly.

Dr. George took Cubby's hands and folded them into his own. "My mother and I would hold hands, and we'd say:

Dear Lord,
We thank you for our many, many blessings. Please grant us faith, courage, kindness, love, and understanding.
Amen.

"Amen," repeated Cubby. "I like that. Say it again."

Dr. George repeated it several times until Cubby had memorized it, until Dr. George could almost feel his mother in the room. He closed his eyes and saw her smiling proudly. Her son, the doctor, was passing on their special prayer.

Saying good night, Dr. George stepped softly toward the closet doorway. Cubby called after him, "Pops, should I say a prayer for Mrs. Helling and her baby?"

"That would be nice," Dr. George said, quietly closing the door partway.

"And Pops?"

"Yes, Cubby?"

"I'm glad I'm with you. I love you, Pops."

Dr. George stiffened. Emotions rushed over him, emotions he hadn't felt for a long time. He wanted to reach out, wanted to tell Cubby he loved him, too, but the words wouldn't come.

So he simply said, "Thank you, Cubby. I'm glad you're here also."

As he walked to his reading chair, he wondered why he couldn't say *I love you* to Cubby.

CHAPTER 8

RABBIT'S FOOT

The Younguns couldn't have been any happier with the snow, because school had been cancelled until after Thanksgiving. Sherry was quiet and didn't talk as much as usual, which pleased her brothers, Larry and Terry.

Rev. Youngun had given them a lecture on how animals had been created for people to eat, but it hadn't gone well. Terry had asked, "Were dogs made for us to eat?"

Rev. Youngun said, "Korean people eat dogs, but we . . ."

Ten-year-old Larry interrupted him, "What kind of dogs? Great Danes, German shepherds?"

"I'm not sure what kinds of dogs they . . ."

Terry stopped him, "Hold it, Pa. How do they cook 'em? Do they fry 'em? Do they barbeque 'em?"

"You'd need a big barbeque spit to hold a Great Dane," Larry said, "wouldn't ya, Pa?"

Terry raised his hand. "Pa, how do they get the hair off a poodle? Or do they just eat hairless dogs like those Mexican jumpin' bean dogs?"

Rev. Youngun was at a loss for words. "Mexican jumping bean dogs? What are those?"

Larry spoke up. "He means chi-wa-was. You know those dogs that look like rats that the migrant laborers have."

"I'll have one order of fried Saint Bernard with a mutt sandwich on the side," Terry screamed, startling everyone. "Think they'd want to eat Dangit?" he laughed, kicking the dog awake. Dangit the dog growled from under the table. Terry kicked at him. "Hush, dummy, nobody'd eat your scrawny body anyway!"

Rev. Youngun tried a bait-and-switch. "Did you read the article in the newspaper about the circus elephant that got loose in St. Louis and . . ."

Larry jumped in. "Do people eat elephants?"

Rev. Youngun tried to regain control of the conversation. "Hush. Please, children, listen!" A temporary silence prevailed. "Did you know that in Africa they eat elephants and . . ."

Larry screamed out, "Uhhhhhhh, yuuuuck! Can you imagine eatin' an elephant's trunk?"

"Pa, why does an elephant need a suitcase?" Sherry asked.

"He's talkin' 'bout the elephant's nose, you dummy," Terry snapped, sticking his tongue out.

"That's right," Rev. Youngun stammered, "the elephant's trunk is his long snout, which they cut into pieces and . . ."

"Pa, I don't like this kind of talk!" Sherry screamed.

Terry made a face and stuck out his tongue, "You know what you'd like?" he asked Sherry.

"Don't tell me!" she pouted, holding her hands over her ears.

Terry ignored her, "You'd like to eat cooked elephant's rump roast. Pa could set it on the table and it'd be so big that you could stand inside the elephant's cooked rump and eat your way out!"

Sherry began crying and Rev. Youngun looked dumbfounded. Larry and Terry were laughing so hard that tears came to their eyes.

Sherry was disgusted with the whole conversation, and when

she found they were having rabbit for dinner, she refused to eat. "I won't eat a bunny rabbit," she said defiantly.

"Sherry, I told you that some animals are raised for food, and some animals are raised for pets," said Rev. Youngun.

"Bunny rabbits are pets, not food," she said, crossing her arms.

Terry ran into the kitchen and came back hopping into the dining room with a carrot in his mouth singing, "Here comes Peter Cottontail, hopping down the bunny trail."

Sherry screamed as he hopped up to her chair and laid his lucky rabbit's foot on her plate. Larry then completely ruined her appetite by saying loudly, "Let's eat, Pa. I want a big piece of Peter rabbit!"

After dinner, Sherry went to Larry's room. "What's goin' to happen to Teddy Roosevelt?"

"I overheard Pa talkin' about makin' Teddy Roosevelt into Thanksgiving dinner. We got to think of somethin'."

Terry came into the room, wearing his favorite nightshirt, which looked like a throwaway with all the rips and stains. "Mr. Springer says that if we come to the turkey tree with him, we might find another turkey and save T.R.'s neck from Pa's axe!"

"Turkey tree? What's that?" Sherry asked.

"I never heard of it either," Terry said, "but Mr. Springer says it's a tree where you shoot up in the air and a turkey falls out."

"Wish they had a candy tree," Sherry said.

"When is he takin' us to the turkey tree?" Larry asked.

"Sometime tomorrow." Terry closed the door and whispered, "Maybe we should put a hoodoo on anyone who tries to kill T.R."

"What's a hoodoo?" whispered Sherry.

"A hoodoo's a curse, like writin' the name of your enemy twelve times on a piece of paper, then burnin' the paper with a candle to start trouble against that person."

"How do you know if a hoodoo works?" asked Larry.

"Easy, a mark appears somewhere on the person's body, you know like 'X marks the spot' and all that," said Terry, arching his eyebrows.

"You know how to do that?" Larry whispered carefully.

"Sure, I listen to the field workers over in the holler. They don't know I'm listenin'. That's how I learned 'bout this kind of neat stuff," Terry said proudly.

"Those people are sellin' their souls to the devil?" Larry asked.

"They talk 'bout how to do it, that's all," Terry said, trying to get out of the mess he'd put himself in.

"How do you sell your gold to the devil?" Sherry whispered.

"Soul, not gold, you knothead!" Terry walked over to the closed door and listened. Fractured moonlight, piercing through the falling snow, created an eerie effect on the walls of the room.

Terry looked into their eyes, "A hoodoo man only gets his powers when he sells his soul to the devil. That's why they have Devil's Ridge outside town. It's where the hoodoo men go on the darkest night of the month, all alone, waiting for him to appear."

"Him who?" whispered Sherry, all wide-eyed and frightened.

"The devil!" he exclaimed, bopping her on the head.

Larry grabbed his hand. "Don't hit girls."

Looking up into his older, bigger, and stronger brother's eyes, Terry shrugged his arm off. "Sorry, forgot she was a girl. Anyway, at the stroke of midnight, the devil takes the shape of a blackbird and comes up to the hoodoo man to strike the deal for the hoodoo man's soul."

"Don't believe any of that," declared Sherry, shaking her head.

"Did you know that last night a hoodoo man lost his big toe?" Terry asked, eyeing her big toe sticking out from the blanket.

"Did he find it?" Sherry whispered.

"No, but I heard him outside tonight, wandering around, crying out," Terry paused and said in his best monster voice, "Where is my toe . . . where is my toe?"

The wind rattled the door and Sherry grabbed on to Larry, "What's that?" she whispered.

"That's him! He wants his toe back," Terry whispered. He walked over to the door and moaned in the same voice, "Where is my toe?"

Terry pulled the door open and shouted in his monster voice, "There it is!" and grabbed Sherry's big toe.

She screamed and fell off the bed. Larry raised his eyebrows and pointed toward the doorway.

Terry ignored him. "There's no one outside the door, Larry, no one except maybe the hoodoo man," Terry said, turning and pointing to the doorway. His father was standing there. "Oh, hi, Pa."

"I came up to find out why you didn't clean up your room like I asked you."

Terry shook his head like a dog waving a bone around. "I don't need a clean room. I like it the way it is."

Rev. Youngun loudly clapped his hands together to get attention. "I don't like it! It looks like a pig's sty!"

Terry wailed, "I don't need a room! Just fill it with rocks and board it up. Fill it full of cement. I don't need a room. I'll sleep in the barn."

Rev. Youngun pulled Terry from the room to clean up his mess. Larry sneaked out quietly, leaving Sherry lying there whimpering.

Soon Rev. Youngun came in. "What's wrong? Did Terry scare you with the hoodoo talk?"

"No," she sniffled, "you said pig's sty . . . that reminded me of Bessie."

"I'm sorry, I . . ."

"I want her back, Pa. I do."

"You'll get over it," he said, laying her back down. "There'll be other animals you'll love."

"There'll never be another Bessie," she whispered, snuggling into her blam-blam and sucking her thumb.

CHAPTER 9

POLLY, WANNA CRACKER?

Another four inches of snow fell during the night. A new calf that dropped before dawn froze to death at the Rikala's farm. With the roads barely passable, the churches set up sleeping quarters for some of the elderly in the rectory buildings.

Eulla Mae Springer had invited Dr. George over to their house so she could meet Cubby. She had also invited her sister Polly, who had an angel's smile and was shaped like a pear.

Polly giggled and laughed at everything Dr. George said, which was very flattering, except that he wasn't looking to get married.

Eulla Mae handed him a plate of greens and asked pointedly, "Polly, did you know that Dr. George is the only black doctor in Missouri?"

Polly looked at Dr. George and smiled. Dr. George blushed.

"Look at that, Eulla Mae," Maurice laughed. "I ain't never seen a black man blush."

Dr. George blushed even deeper, and Polly giggled louder.

Eulla Mae looked sternly at her husband. "Hush that! Black people blush, 'cause blushin's a state of mind."

Maurice chuckled to himself. "I'm so black you can't see *my* state of mind when I blush."

Polly giggled and looked over at Dr. George, batting her eyes, doing everything her sister had told her to do.

Eulla Mae was playing Cupid; she wanted a doctor married into the family. She shook her head at Dr. George. "It must be hard, raisin' Cubby all by yourself." Before he could respond, Eulla Mae reached over and patted Cubby on the head. "Is he bein' a good papa to you?"

Cubby smiled, "Peep . . ." He caught himself at the same time he caught the harsh glare from Dr. George. "Pops is very good to me. He lets me sleep in his clothes closet in an old wagon seat he made into a bed for me."

Eulla Mae frowned. "You sleep in a clothes closet? Dr. George, you need to buy you a bigger house, and . . ." she paused, looking over at her sister, "you need a good woman like Polly."

Maurice burst out laughing. Cubby smiled, and Polly turned her face away in embarrassment. Dr. George sat there blushing like a schoolboy. For the rest of the meal, he tried to avoid Eulla Mae's looks and hints. He was only too relieved when the meal ended and the women went to do the dishes.

In the kitchen, Eulla Mae smiled at her chubby sister. "How do you like him?"

Polly smiled and dried off another dish, "He's very nice and very handsome."

Eulla Mae put her hands on her sister's shoulders. "Girl, you're never goin' to get a man if all you do is giggle. This man's a doctor! He's educated!"

Polly started to giggle again, then caught herself. "What do I do?" she asked in a high-pitched voice.

"You have to talk. I told you that!"

"Talk about what?" Polly asked, looking down.

"Talk about doctorin' or the weather or how handsome he is. You know how to talk to men, don't you?"

"I never talked to a man about things like that," Polly said, closing her eyes. "Boys always called me Fatbird Polly in school."

"I know, girl, I know," Eulla Mae said, hugging Polly. "But there comes a time at least once in every woman's life when she has the chance to blossom."

"There does?" Polly asked hopefully.

"Sure does. Every woman gets at least one chance to come out like a butterfly and grab a memory for life. Some get married; some don't. But you got to grab that chance when it comes around."

"I'll try, Sis. I'll try," she whispered, looking down.

Eulla Mae hugged her again. "After we finish the dishes, you go on into the parlor with the men and you listen for your chance to say somethin'."

While Cubby played by himself in the bedroom, Maurice and Dr. George talked in the parlor. Maurice asked, "How you like Polly?"

Dr. George stood at the parlor window and looked out at the falling snow. "Oh, she's all right. She'll make some man a good wife."

"Eulla Mae wants to make her your wife," Maurice chuckled.

"Well, she's nice, but I think she's just a few pounds overweight."

Maurice threw back his hands. "A few pounds? Why, I'd say she was a few hundred pounds overweight!" He laughed, then caught himself, looking toward the women in the kitchen. He walked over to Dr. George and asked, in a conspiratorial tone, "You know what Polly is short for?"

Dr. George shook his head and guessed, "Pollyanna?"

"No," Maurice grinned slyly. "It's short for pollywog. You know, like the frog."

Dr. George got into the mood. "I thought she was named for a parrot."

"A parrot?" Maurice snickered.

Dr. George laughed quietly. "Yeah, you know, like 'Polly wanna cracker?' "

They both laughed loudly. "No," Maurice said, trying to hold back his tears. "Polly don't wanna cracker. Polly wanna the whole box!" Maurice guffawed, slapping his leg.

"Polly would eat the box too!" Dr. George laughed.

Behind them, Polly stood in the doorway, tears streaming down her face. She'd heard it all.

Maurice and Dr. George noticed her at the same time and straightened up. Both men were blushing with humiliation.

Maurice stammered, "Polly, I'm sorry. We were . . ."

Polly, who hadn't spoken a word during dinner, interrupted. "You're not sorry. Neither of you are. All my life people have made fun of me. Called me Fatbird, Chubby, Piggy-piggy."

Eulla Mae came up, glaring at her husband. She put her arm around Polly. "You come with me, Polly."

Polly shook her off. "You said my chance would come, and it did. It slapped me in the face!" She walked over to Dr. George and put her finger to his nose. "Just 'cause you're educated and a doctor don't 'scuse your bad manners."

She looked toward Maurice and back to Dr. George. "I may be fat, but I'd rather be fat than mean."

Polly stormed out of the room, leaving the two men speechless. Maurice stammered, "Eulla Mae, I . . ."

Eulla Mae wagged her finger at them both. "Don't say you didn't say it, 'cause you said it. You can't change words once they're spoken!"

Dr. George looked down and said quietly, "I'm sorry for hurtin' your sister's feelings, Eulla Mae. Cubby and I best be goin' home now." He got Cubby from the bedroom and quietly put their coats on. Maurice waved good-bye as the sleigh slipped past the porch. Dr. George maneuvered the sleigh through the frozen darkness, his cheeks still burning with embarrassment. He was so ashamed of himself.

He'd complained about Manly and Maurice making fun of

other people, told Cubby not to let people pick on him, and bristled with anger at Jacob Helling's prejudice against him. *I'm a hypocrite, a first-class hypocrite,* he thought to himself. Cracking the whip in the crisp air, Dr. George could feel the shame in his soul. He had humiliated Polly for no reason at all. Dr. George had refused to see Polly as a person and had treated her as he wouldn't want to be treated himself.

He thought back to his mother telling him, "People are people. They all have a heart that can be hurt. Just treat others as you want to be treated, and you'll get along with everyone."

Tonight he had let his mother down.

CHAPTER 10

IS ROSE COMING?

Laura stood on the front porch, wrapping a shawl tightly around her shoulders. Though she could hardly see the barn through the falling snow, she peered down the drive.

Manly came out onto the porch and stood beside her, wiping snow off the rail. "Come on in, Laura. It's too cold to stand out here."

"The telegram said Rose left school two days ago. She should be here by now," Laura said.

Manly put his sweatered arm around her. "She'll be all right," he said, but he didn't sound convinced himself. "I asked the sheriff to put the word out in the south county. There'll be a whole string of folks lookin' out for her."

A gust of wind picked up the snow on the porch and whirled it around them. Laura shivered and held her arms. "It looks as if this is going to be a hard winter."

"If the snow keeps up, it'll block all the roads."

Laura blew snow off her nose. "I remember the winter of 1880, when it stayed forty below."

Manly shivered with the memory. "Snowdrifts were forty feet

deep from December until May." He paused, blinking snow off his eyelids. "Some good folks died that year. Froze to death without wood."

"You risked your life even going outside your door," Laura said quietly.

Manly stamped his feet to warm them. "Worst part was the hoarding. Last sack of flour in town sold for fifty bucks. Sugar was more than a buck a pound."

Laura laid her head on his shoulder. "And you and your brother drove fifteen miles through the blizzard to buy seed wheat so the children could have bread."

"And we ground the wheat in the coffee grinder."

"That was a hard winter. Tough times." She lifted her head off his shoulder and looked at him. "You call Rev. Youngun and tell him about the apple?" Laura asked.

"I stopped by and told him. He asked Sherry if she'd snuck back over and left an apple on the rail by Bessie's pen, and she said she had." Manly brushed a large snowflake off his nose. "That girl asked me if I'd buried Bessie's bones and put a cross over 'em. Can you imagine that?"

Laura sighed. "I put a cross over my pets' graves when I was little. I understand how she feels, but for her it's worse."

"How so?"

"We didn't eat my pets," she said, stamping her feet. "I'm feeling kind of tired from worrying about Rose, Manly. Let's have some magnolia tea to perk up."

"I'll just have some black coffee. I'm cold down to my bones."

The door closed behind them, locking out the bitter cold of the hard winter that had come again.

In the hollow outside of town, Martha Helling called, "Get Dr. George for me, Jacob. Please!"

With a grunt, Jacob shoved another log into the cookstove to warm the room, then stood back, warming himself.

"Please. It hurts, Jacob."

He took a cold cloth and wiped the fever sweats from her forehead. "You'll be all right. My momma delivered me by herself. Indian women do it. You just got spoiled on me." Putting down the cloth, he dipped a spoon into an earthen bowl. "Here, eat this."

She made a face. "Jacob, I can't eat any more raw garlic."

"Chopped garlic's what the folk healers recommend for everything. It cures the blood of ailments."

Swallowing deeply, she puckered her nose to the smell. "If I eat anymore, I'm goin' to be sick." A shudder went through her body and she shut her eyes at the pain. "Can you get me a midwife? Please?"

"There's a Catholic midwife who only works on folks in the Hardacres. We don't need her in our home."

Martha drank slowly from the cup of water by the bed. "What 'bout Miss Sue? She birthed a lot of the babies 'round here."

Jacob refilled the cup. "I told you, she moved to Arkansas. Followed after some widowed tent preacher."

Martha looked with pleading eyes to her husband. "Dr. George is a doctor. You got to let him attend to me, Jacob. You got to."

"I'd rather see you die."

Another blast of pain shot up her spine. "You just might get your wish, Jacob. Then you can bury me yourself."

Jacob momentarily lost his rigid self-control. He rushed from the house, into the snowstorm.

In the same snowstorm, over a hundred miles away, Rose Wilder was standing on the deck of the *Mississippi Queen,* the finest riverboat of its day. Her friend, Mary Lou Tibleaux, shivered against the cold. The lights of Memphis flickered through the snow ahead.

They'd come by Mary Lou's Oldsmobile as far as Baton Rouge, Louisiana, but the car had broken down. The blacksmith and part-time auto mechanic said it'd take at least two weeks to fix, so with Thanksgiving just days away, they'd talked their way onto the *Mississippi Queen*.

Their plan was to get off at Cairo, Illinois, and take the train to Springfield, Missouri, getting off at Mansfield. The only problem with their plan was the weather.

The captain of the *Mississippi Queen* had told Rose that the last sounder in Greenville, Mississippi, had yelled up the news that the Memphis to Little Rock rail line had been closed. Snowdrifts between Forrest City and Brinkley, Arkansas, had made it all but impassable.

If the train was stopped there, no telling what it was like in the isolated forest areas approaching Mansfield. Some of the smaller towns probably had no snow-moving equipment at all, except for shovels and strong backs.

The blasting boat whistle woke up the night, and deck and cabin hands scurried about as the Memphis dock loomed into view. Mary Lou Tibleaux turned and asked, "Think we'll make it to your house for Thanksgiving?"

"We've come this far. There's no turning back now."

Mary Lou shook her head. "I think we should have stayed with my folks in New Orleans. We could have gone to all the dances."

Rose turned to Mary Lou. "I've got to get home. I can't explain why, but I think my mother needs me."

Mary Lou brushed snow from her hair. "All mothers want their daughters back. It's a way of not having to deal with their husbands."

The dance band struck up its traditional fast-paced, good-bye-going-ashore-number, the same one they played at each port of call. Mary Lou spun around, dancing with herself.

Rose set her jaw. "My mother's not like that. She was raised on the prairie and loves my father."

"Oh, darling, we Gibson girls just love to dance! Wagons are so gauche!" Mary Lou laughed, blowing kisses to her imaginary beaux.

Rose was flustered. "You wouldn't understand! She was part of something that changed America."

"Who cares? Wagons, immigrants, horses—I don't know why I let you talk me into going to Mis-sour-ree with you," Mary Lou said, drawing out the syllables.

"You'll like my folks, and you'll love Apple Hill Farm. Did you know that when we arrived in Missouri from the Dakota Territory in our wagon, we only had one hundred dollars to our name?"

"Please, please," Mary Lou said with a dramatic swirl, "not another wagon story. I'm tired of hearing about your mother's pioneer days. Why doesn't she write a book about it, if it was so great?"

"Maybe she will. Maybe she will," Rose said, looking toward the lights of Memphis, wishing she had come alone on this journey home.

CHAPTER 11

TURKEY TREE

Maurice had a hard time keeping a straight face as he and his band of hunters marched along in the snow. The only real rifle in the bunch was the shotgun in his hands, but the "guns" that the Younguns were carrying seemed just as real to them.

Larry took the lead with his broom-pole rifle. Terry marched right behind him, moving his arm like a soldier, the rest of the broom in his hands.

Bringing up the rear was little Sherry, who could hardly walk because she was so bundled up against the cold. Nevertheless, she did her best, marching along, holding her blam-blam blankey in one hand and a long kitchen spoon in the other.

Her feet moved up and down like a regular little soldier, and her dolly, Carrie Nation, peeked out from inside her coat. Every so often she'd sneak her thumb into her mouth for a little suck. Larry had helped her slit the thumb of her right glove so she could suck on the thumb without the rest of her hand getting cold.

Maurice looked behind him and laughed again. He'd been marching around in circles for over an hour, trying to wear them out. They were so confused as to where they were that they had no idea where they were going. "Troops, halt!" Maurice said, holding up his hand.

The three Younguns bumped into one another. Larry went face first into the snow. Terry landed on top of Larry, and Sherry was knocked on her rump. A pine branch, heavy with snow, dipped downward and dumped its snow on her head. The boys laughed when Sherry burst out crying.

Maurice walked over. "Quit your cryin', girl." He reached out his hand and pulled her up, then whispered, "We's approachin' the turkey tree."

The three Younguns were wide-eyed. "We are?" asked Larry.

Maurice put his finger to his lips, "Sh. You'll wake the turkey tree up."

As he looked up and around, six Youngun eyes followed his gaze. Maurice had picked out a tall pine tree that he'd climbed as a boy. It was next to a huge boulder jutting out from the hill south of his farm. When he was a young boy, he and his friends would come camp out under the boulder's ledge, telling stories by campfire.

It was on one of those camping trips that the turkey tree was discovered. Mansfield used to have turkey drives through the center of town right before Thanksgiving and Christmas. Six hundred and fifty turkeys were once walked through town in a drove. To Maurice, it was like watching six hundred and fifty Christmas dinners strolling past him, each one ready to be dressed for dinner.

But the gobblers' march soon turned into a feathered mess as a pack of wild dogs jumped from an alley into the middle of the drove. The women ran screaming for cover while the men fought back the dogs with sticks.

By the time they'd beaten the dogs back, the turkeys were scattered throughout the town. A few dozen mysteriously disappeared, though the hotel restaurant had a special on turkey suppers the next day.

The day after the big turkey drive, Maurice and his friends were out camping by the big pine tree. Maurice wanted to play a joke and took out his shotgun and stood under the tree. He intended to fire it into the air to scare his friends.

He scared his friends, all right, but he also scared himself! Seconds after he pulled the trigger, a big turkey fell from the tree, landing right on top of him. Seems that several turkeys from the drive were hiding out in the pine tree. He and his friends used the rest of the shells and bagged themselves Christmas dinner. From that day forward, Maurice and his friends called that pine the turkey tree.

To help the Younguns save their turkey, Teddy Roosevelt, from the Thanksgiving axe, Maurice had come out to the tree earlier in the morning and tied one of his own turkeys up on a branch. *Sometimes legends need a little bit of help,* he'd chuckled to himself.

"Okay, little Younguns, we found the turkey tree." Their eyes followed his pointing finger to the tree, and then all looked up toward the top. It was a very tall pine tree.

"That's the biggest Christmas tree I've ever seen," said Sherry, shaking her head.

"That's not a Christmas tree. That's the turkey tree. There's a big difference," said Maurice.

"What's the difference?" Larry asked.

Maurice dusted snow off his shoulders. "Well, a turkey tree has turkeys in it, and a Christmas tree has Christmas on it." Larry just stared, without saying anything. "Did you understand me?" Maurice asked.

"Didn't make any sense to me at all," Larry said.

"How do we get the turkeys to come down?" asked Terry.

"You gotta have the right trot," Maurice deadpanned.

"Not me!" said Terry. "I don't ever want to have the trots again! Thought my fanny was goin' to fall off!"

Maurice shook his head, "No, no, no! I ain't talkin' 'bout

having the trots and sittin' in the outhouse all day. I'm talkin' 'bout doin' *the trot.*"

"The what?" asked Larry.

Maurice leaned his rifle against the boulder. "The trot. The turkey trot. You got to trot if you want the turkey to come down."

He began dancing around, flapping his arms as if they were wings. He moved his head up and down and gobbled like a turkey. "Think you can do the turkey trot?" he asked.

"You look pretty silly, Mr. Springer," said Larry.

Maurice didn't miss a beat. "Sometimes you got to do silly things in this life to make something wonderful happen."

Maurice spun around and gobbled loudly into the air. "Come on, do it. If you don't do the turkey trot, ol' Teddy Roosevelt's head's gonna be flopping on the ground come Thanksgiving morning."

The three children hesitated, then Terry took the first step. With his auburn hair bouncing around, he looked like a barn-yard rooster. Larry finally jumped up and down, gobbling, and then Sherry did a very petite chicken-scratch sort of dance. Soon they were all dancing and gobbling.

Maurice thought this was just about the funniest thing he'd ever talked these kids into doing. He danced around and shouted, "Keep up the turkey trot and repeat after me."

Using the cadence of a military drill song, Maurice called out, "Hey there, turkey in the tree."

The Younguns shouted back in unison, "Hey there, turkey in the tree."

"A Thanksgiving dinner you soon will be."

"A Thanksgiving dinner you soon will be," the Younguns repeated.

Maurice jumped up and down. "Cookin' in the oven's goin' be your fate."

The Younguns shouted back, "Cookin' in the oven's goin' be your fate."

Maurice licked his fingers. "Goin' lick my fingers and wipe my plate."

"Goin' lick my fingers and wipe my plate," they yelled back. Sherry stuck her thumb in her mouth.

Maurice was having a royal time of it. He had the three Younguns following him around, circling the base of the tree. Finally, he raised his hand and said, "Okay, it's time to see if we get lucky."

The loud growl of a bobcat silenced them. The three kids grabbed Maurice's leg. "What was that?" Terry whispered.

"Where's my gun?" Maurice whispered. It was sitting against the rock, and with the three kids holding onto his legs, he struggled getting over to it.

The bobcat growled again. "Is that a lion?" Sherry whispered, eyes as wide as saucers.

Maurice put his fingers to his lips. "Sounds like a bobcat to me. Wonder what he's doin'?" His question was answered as enough feathers to fill a pillow came floating down from the tree. His eyes followed the feathers' trail until he spotted the bobcat, sitting on a branch, his jaws full of the turkey Maurice had conveniently tied to the branch for him.

"Looks like that old bobcat got here first," said Larry, shaking his head sadly.

"This is curtains for Teddy Roosevelt," whimpered Terry. He pulled out his pocketknife and opened the blade. "I'll keep that old bobcat away. I'll do it," he whispered. With a parting growl, the bobcat bounded out of the tree, turkey gripped in his mouth, and loped off up the hill.

Maurice knelt down in the snow and looked into their eyes. "I'm sorry, children. I'm really sorry. I was hopin' that you could get a turkey from the turkey tree and save Teddy Roosevelt."

Terry interrupted him. "Why did the Pilgrims have to eat a turkey? It would have been better if they'd all sat down to a squirrel pie or a bag of Tootsie rolls."

Maurice grinned. "Some people serve duck or roast chicken or a baked ham."

Sherry gasped, "I'm *never* goin' to eat ham again! It could be Bessie!"

Larry scratched his head. "Where do people get a turkey if they don't have a turkey livin' in their yard?"

"They go to the butcher shop. Butchers always got lots of turkeys hangin' in the cold room before holidays."

An idea hit Terry like a ton of bricks. He had a way to save T.R.'s neck! "We best be gettin' on home, Mr. Springer," Terry said. "Pa's expectin' us." He looked up the hill toward the bobcat and held his knife up. "That cat's lucky I didn't climb up there and cut him up good!"

Maurice looked at the open knife Terry was swinging around. "Give me that knife, boy!"

Terry put it behind his back. "No, please, this is my favorite thing in the whole world!"

"Then put it away, *now!*" Maurice snapped. "You can hurt someone with that."

Terry folded up the blade and slipped it into his jacket pocket, not realizing there was a hole in it. His pocketknife fell into the snow, gone for good.

Maurice stood and picked up his shotgun. "You want me to look for another turkey tree in the mornin'? Thanksgivin' dinner's not till tomorrow afternoon."

"No, that's all right. You tried, Mr. Springer," Larry said, picking up his stick rifle.

Maurice marched them back toward their home. "Not everything works out every time. That's just the way things is in this ol' world."

"I wish this ol' world had candy trees," Terry muttered.

Maurice laughed. "You just gotta believe. All things are possible."

Sherry pulled at his pants leg. "Mr. Springer? Mr. Springer?"

Maurice stopped. "Yes, child?"

"Do you think lyin's bad?"

"Tellin' a lie is breakin' one of the Ten Commandments," he said.

"Do you always tell the truth?" she asked, looking him straight in the eye.

Maurice knew something was up. Sherry had a way of leading you down a blind alley with her questions until your back was to the wall. Maurice picked her up in his arms. "Sure I do, girl. I'm a religious man."

"Tell me the truth," she said seriously. "Is Santa real?"

Larry and Terry looked at him, waiting for the answer. Sherry was five and Terry was seven, so they certainly believed in the magic of Christmas. Larry was ten, so if he believed, this might be the last Christmas he did so.

"Is Santa real?" Sherry asked again.

Maurice put Sherry back on the ground and patted the boys on their heads. "Is Santa real, you ask me? You know the answer to that, don't you?" he said, grinning.

"He's real!" Sherry screamed. "I knew it!"

A look of relief swept over the boys' faces. "You had me worried there for a moment, Mr. Springer," Larry said.

"Yeah," piped Terry. "I thought you were going to tell me that it was Pa I saw in the living room last year. Looked like him, it did."

Terry paused in thought. "Does Santa have helpers? 'Cause this Santa was kind of skinny."

"Maybe he just hadn't eaten the cookies you'd left out for him," Maurice said, smiling.

"He couldn't!" Sherry exclaimed.

"Why, child?" Maurice asked.

"'Cause Terry ate 'em!" she said, pointing to her brother.

Maurice burst out laughing, and they began their march again.. After traveling a hundred yards or so, Terry called out, "Hey, Mr. Springer."

"Yes, Terry?" Maurice asked.

Terry spoke with the innocence of a child. "I heard the men at the barbershop say that white people are afraid to go into some of the bad areas of St. Louis."

"That's probably true. 'Course there's black men who are frightened to go into some bad areas, too."

"Well, Mr. Springer," Terry began, "I was just wonderin'. Santa is a big, fat white man in a red suit, carryin' a bag of toys. Isn't he worried 'bout goin' into a bad neighborhood?"

Maurice stopped and turned to look at the three of them. "Who says Santa's white?"

Larry had a perplexed look on his face. "Gosh, Mr. Springer. All the books show him as a white man."

Maurice shook his head. " 'Cause the books are drawn by white men thinkin' 'bout a fat white man. Ain't that true?"

"I've never seen a black Santa," said Larry.

"Santa Claus sounds like a white person's name to me," cracked Terry.

"Probably German or Swedish," Larry said, very matter-of-factly.

Maurice stood up straight, closed one eye and bent over toward the boys. "Do you know what Santa's middle name is?"

Larry and Terry shook their heads. "No, Mr. Springer," they said in unison.

Sherry pleaded, "What's Santa's middle name? What's his middle name?"

Maurice straightened up and grinned. "Santa's middle name is Lemuel. Santa Lemuel Claus. Only black men named Lemuel. You think 'bout it."

"Maybe he's light," said Sherry, "like Dr. George."

"Dr. George would make a good Santa," Larry added.

"Why?" Maurice asked quietly.

Larry said matter-of-factly, " 'Cause he's a good man and helps the poor people without chargin' 'em."

Maurice nodded and marched them back to their home, deep

in thought. *Why do I like to pick on Dr. George? Am I jealous of his education? Of his light color?*

At the back of the line, Terry whispered to Larry, "I got an idea on how we're goin' to save Teddy Roosevelt. You got any money hidden away? I got some in my jacket pocket."

Terry reached in, and his hand came out through the hole. "My knife! I've lost my knife! We've got to find it."

"It's gone, son," Maurice said, shaking his head. He looked back at their tracks through the deep snow. "We'll never find it. It's lost in the snow someplace."

"But I want another one!" Terry whined.

"Ask Santa," Sherry answered.

"Yeah," said Maurice, "ask Santa Lemuel Claus. Maybe he can get you another one."

CHAPTER 12

ROOTS

ose and Mary Lou Tibleaux agreed to part company at Cairo, Illinois. The snide comments of her friend made Rose truly appreciate her own roots.

Perhaps Rose had been blinded by the clothes and attitudes of the wealthy girls at her exclusive New Orleans school. She'd tried to fit in, to become a Gibson girl, emulating the latest fashion rage, and had taken to thinking that riding in anything less than a brand-new car was beneath her.

Waving good-bye to Mary Lou at the boat dock, Rose knew that things have a way of working out for the best. Mary Lou was able to get on the last boat bound for New Orleans, and would spend the holidays with her own folks.

You can't change the past, and the events of her mother's life, and of her own, were worth more than all the money and fancy parties in the world. The simple things Mary Lou had made fun of now took on special meaning for Rose.

Rose was coming into her own as a woman; she could see through the vanity and pretentions of the Mary Lou Tibleaux crowd. How they'd probably laughed behind her back as she told about her prairie upbringing in her first days of classes. Why hadn't she seen through their false smiles?

Mary Lou was the most popular girl in school, and Rose wanted to be accepted. When Mary Lou took Rose under her wing to show her the latest fads and help her fit in, Rose couldn't have been happier.

As a matter of fact, Rose wondered why Mary Lou had even wanted to come to Apple Hill Farm for Thanksgiving. Was she on a dare, or was it just another one of her larks?

Rose had been an eager follower, looking for guidance from Mary Lou. She'd learned the dances and copied her clothes. Rose had even tried to match the New Orleans aristocratic accent of the "planter's class."

Rose had tried so hard to be like them that she had forgotten who she was and where she'd come from. She had learned from her parents to survive hardship and heartache. She could remember her baby brother being buried on the barren Dakota plains. Life was a fragile, special thing.

The fire and lost crops had brought them together as a family, because they had only themselves left. She had memories of crossing the Dakotas and coming down through the prairies of mid-America into Missouri. She had memories of starting life from scratch and, through hard work, of building something to be proud of.

Setting out for the train station, Rose now knew that she wouldn't trade their farmhouse for the finest mansion in New Orleans. What she and her parents had built was special, because they'd built it with their own hands.

Never again would she allow others to mock her past as if it were without meaning and not worthy of comment. Rose had what the wealthy girls at school would never have—stamina and fortitude derived from hard work, thrift, and faith.

You could take everything away from some people, and they would never be able to get back up. But if a person has stamina, fortitude, and faith, he could move mountains.

Survival took roots—not like Mary Lou's family line, which supposedly went all the way to France, but the roots of your parents and their values, shared experiences, and a feeling of being wanted.

Rose had it all. She had real roots.

Rose took the buggy cab from the port to the train station and managed to get the last train that evening heading toward Springfield. Mansfield was the next-to-last stop, which would give her time to rest.

Settling down into her seat, she fell into a deep sleep. She dreamed of being in a wagon on the road to Missouri, a dream better than any nickel movie she'd ever seen.

While Rose was dreaming her way toward Mansfield, Laura was worried sick about her daughter. With the snowdrifts building up and reports of the back roads being closed, Laura couldn't sleep or eat.

Manly was worried, too, but he knew there was nothing he could do about it.

"Manly, do you think Rose will make it home for Thanksgiving?" Laura asked sadly.

"I just hope she makes it home." Manly gazed out the window, remembering the winter of '81 when the snow fell forty-seven feet deep on the railroad tracks.

Laura walked over to Manly and they clung together tightly, trying to hug their fears away.

CHAPTER 13

BUTCHER, BAKER, BABYMAKER

The snow fell heavily during the night. Notices were posted in town that most of the phone lines were down. The telegraph still worked to Springfield, though not to Little Rock.

Manly shoveled the snow off the front and back stairs, while Laura prepared the turkey he'd killed at dawn. As he worked, the thought of Laura's turkey and dressing was enough to warm him against the bitter cold.

Dr. George stopped by before noon, on his way with Cubby to share Thanksgiving at the Springers' house. Cubby went with Manly to see the animals in the barn while Dr. George talked with Laura. Over a cup of coffee, he poured his heart out about Martha Helling's worsening condition.

"She needs a doctor, but her husband's a stubborn old mule," Dr. George said, shaking his head.

"Maybe he'll change his mind at the last minute. When's the baby due?" Laura asked.

"Not for 'bout another month, but it might come any time."

"I wish I could help you in some way," Laura said sincerely.

"You can," Dr. George grinned.

"How?" Laura asked.

"You could midwife her baby."

"Midwife? I had trouble delivering my own baby, and I had help! Me, midwife? I don't think so."

Dr. George pressed forward. "Laura, please, just listen to me for a moment. All you'd have to do is what I tell you. You can be my hands."

Laura looked at the doctor. "Why are you so concerned about helping people who don't want your help?"

Dr. George closed his eyes. "Martha Helling has whispered to me that she don't mind that I'm . . ." the necessity of saying this to a friend embarrassed him.

Laura helped him say it. "Black."

"Yes, that I'm a black doctor. But Jacob, he minds. He's been born, bred, and raised on hate."

"It's just so stupid."

Dr. George nodded. "He won't let me touch her." He looked at Laura with pleading eyes. "I need your help. You've got to midwife this baby."

"But I've never birthed a baby before," Laura said quietly.

"Horse feathers! After all the stories I've heard 'bout you and your family criss-crossin' the country in wagons, fightin' Indians and prairie fires, why birthin' babies ought to come natural to you."

Laura walked to the stove and brought back the coffeepot. Refilling their cups, she said, "I'll go visit them with you, and I'll try to talk some sense into Jacob Helling's head."

"That's all I'm askin'."

"I'll go up there, but I'm not promising that I'll midwife the baby for you. I don't know if I want to, or if I could."

"You'll do fine, Laura. I'll be right there with you, to tell you what to do."

Dr. George laughed heartily. "Laura Wilder, if you've pulled the innards from a turkey and stuffed it, you can deliver a baby!"

"I'm glad it's not that simple," she said quietly. "Birthing a baby has got to be harder than just working a turkey like a butcher."

"Why? Ain't much more than that to it."

"Sure it is. 'Cause, if it were that simple, husbands would send their wives to the butcher shop to deliver their babies and pick up a T-bone steak to celebrate with."

Dr. George laughed so hard that coffee dribbled from his mouth, "Sort of like a butcher, baker, and babymaker."

They laughed until they cried. Laura wiped her eyes. "I wonder if the butcher would give a discount for twins?"

CHAPTER 14

GOBBLE-GOBBLE

The Youngun kids' plan to save Teddy Roosevelt had been hurriedly concocted when they found their Pa up at dawn, sharpening his axe against the grinding stone. Sunlight reflected on the razor-sharp blade while Teddy Roosevelt looked from the wooden stall and turned his head.

"Gobble-gobble. Gobble-gobble."

"I'll be with you in a moment, Mr. President," Rev. Youngun said, putting the axe to the stone again. He pumped the foot levers up and down, humming along with the spinning wheel.

"A minister shouldn't be cuttin' off a turkey's head," Larry said over his father's shoulder.

Rev. Youngun kept grinding away. "A minister is also a man, and a man must feed his children."

"A man doesn't have to feed his children Teddy Roosevelt," Sherry whimpered.

"You believe in neighbors helpin' neighbors?" Terry asked.

Rev. Youngun stopped the wheel. "Of course I do. Why?"

Terry was thinking as fast on his feet as ever. " 'Cause Mr. and Mrs. Springer are going to be very disappointed."

Rev. Youngun looked into the eyes of his three children. "Is there something goin' on that I don't know about?"

"No, Pa," Terry began. "It's just that we promised Mr. Springer that he could cut off Teddy Roosevelt's head and gut him and all. And Mrs. Springer . . ." he paused for effect, "She wanted to surprise you by cookin' Teddy Roosevelt in her oven for us."

"She'll be hurt, Pa. She will," said Larry, nodding in agreement.

"Why would they want to do all this for us?" Rev. Youngun asked.

" 'Cause we don't have a momma," Sherry whimpered.

"And they know what a bad cook you are," Terry said without thinking. When he saw the hurt look on his father's face, he looked down. "Sorry, Pa."

Rev. Youngun smiled weakly. "Is my cookin' really that bad, Terry? Go on, tell me the truth."

"Pa," Terry said quietly, "choosin' between eatin' your cookin' and goin' hungry is a choice I think 'bout every meal."

The combination of their thoughts on his cooking, missing their ma, and the fact that it was a holiday convinced him to go along with the children's plan. It saved him from the mess of killing, cleaning, and cooking the turkey.

When he thought about it, it wasn't such a bad deal, after all. He could spend the entire day doing other things. "Tell Mrs. Springer that I sure do appreciate what she's doin' for us." He put away his axe and hitched up the sleigh.

"Where you goin', Pa?" Larry asked.

"I've invited Mr. Johnson to share Thanksgivin' dinner with us."

"Four-Eyes Johnson!" Terry moaned. "He ate with us last year!"

Rev. Youngun nodded. "Yes, but he's all alone and . . ."

Sherry made a face. "And he's got smelly false teeth breath."

"Can't help it that he lost his teeth. Now you children run along and take Teddy Roosevelt over to the Springers."

The Younguns made a big deal of leading Teddy Roosevelt off blindfolded, marching him slowly through the yard, hoping for a reprieve. Each of the Younguns wore a black armband.

Sherry called out to their father, "Say good-bye to Teddy Roosevelt."

"I didn't vote for him," Rev. Youngun laughed.

Terry said, "He'll miss you, Pa. Teddy Roosevelt felt you were kind of like him."

Rev. Youngun turned. "Just like him? Am I a turkey?"

"No," Terry said, "but you're always stickin' your neck out for people and gettin' it chopped off."

"Where'd you hear that?" he asked with a frown.

"That's what I heard you tell Rev. Powers from Springfield. You said your neck's been chopped off, and now Teddy Roosevelt's gonna stick his neck out and have it whacked off."

The mock funeral procession continued around the barn and into the stand of trees about fifty yards back. Once out of sight, they hid behind a log, waiting for their father to leave.

The temperature was dropping, and Sherry grumbled, "My hands are cold! I want to go home!"

"Shush up!" Terry snapped. "We can't go home until Pa leaves."

Sherry made a face. "Thought we were taking Teddy Roosevelt over to the Springers."

Larry tousled her hair. "That was just a story. When Pa leaves we're goin' to hide T.R. in the house."

"But that's fibbin'!" Sherry exclaimed.

"That's right," Terry said, eyeing her. "It's the only way we can save this bird," he said, pointing to T.R., who gobbled back.

Finally Pa left in the sleigh. When he was halfway down the driveway, the three Younguns carried T.R. across the field in a stream of feathers. Once in the house, they hid the turkey in Terry's room. That was about the last place Pa would ever look.

Terry's room was a mess and would stay a mess. Since they knew it gave Pa a headache to even look at the junk heap, they knew it was a safe place to hide T.R.

"Gobble-gobble. Goggle-gobble. Gobble-gobble, gobble-gobble, gobble-gobble."

"If you want to live, you'd better be quiet," snapped Larry.

"Yeah," said Sherry, "if Pa finds you in Terry's room when he gets back, he'll whup us all."

Larry and Sherry sat on the bed, looking at the turkey. "I think he'll be quiet now," Larry said.

Teddy Roosevelt obviously didn't understand. He flapped his wings and let loose with a string of gobble-gobbles.

Terry came through the door, moving his hands up and down for them to be quiet. "You can hear it all over the house. Sounds like a bunch of Pilgrims fightin' over the last turkey at Plymouth Rock." He looked at T.R. flapping his wings and shook his head. "It'll never work."

Sherry tapped T.R. on the beak and placed her finger to her throat. "If you don't be quiet, this is what'll happen to you," she said, pretending to slit her throat.

They felt bad about lying to their father, but they knew that Teddy Roosevelt would have felt much worse if the axe had swung down as planned.

"How long you think Pa will be gone?" Larry asked.

"Enough time for us to get to town and do our business," Terry answered. "You know how Four-Eyes Johnson is. Takes him ten minutes just to find his nose."

Leaving Teddy Roosevelt in Terry's room, the Younguns hitched their extra-long sled behind Crab Apple the mule and headed into Mansfield. Dangit the dog tried to run along beside them, but he kept falling into snowdrifts, so they pulled him onto the sled.

Mansfield was all but shut down, with everyone home, getting ready to sit down for Thanksgiving dinner. Most of the stores, except for the saloon, were closed tight. Crab Apple stopped in front of the butcher shop. There wasn't a light on in front.

"We're in trouble now," moaned Larry.

"We'll have to run away from home," whimpered Sherry.

Terry jumped off and banged on the door. "Open up, Mr. Stevenson. Open up. Rev. Youngun needs you!"

Larry went white. "Terry, don't say that!"

Terry banged on the door again, then turned to his brother. "You think he'd open up on Thanksgivin' Day for a bunch of kids?"

He was interrupted by the creaking door. A lantern was stuck out. "Yes, Rev. Youngun?" the butcher asked, looking above Terry's head.

"It's me, Terry Youngun," said Terry, jumping up to be seen in the light.

Mr. Stevenson lowered the lantern. "What do you want? It's Thanksgiving."

"That's why we're here. It's an emergency. Our pa needs a church turkey quick. He's got some hungry people to feed."

"If he's looking for a free turkey, the answer is no," the butcher said.

"No, we've got money, but we need a turkey we can cook fast."

"Is your father feeding the hungry?" asked the butcher.

"Oh, yes sir! He's feeding some very hungry people. Some very hungry people. One's an old, almost-blind man, and there's some kids who've been near poisoned to death by their daddy's cookin' and. . . ." Terry looked down at his feet, "Our pa needs a turkey he can cook fast 'fore these people starve."

"Can't help you," Mr. Stevenson said, starting to close the door.

Terry stuck his foot in. "Please. You're our only hope."

Sherry began to cry on the sled, and Dangit began howling. A tear slid down Terry's face.

"Come on, Terry," said Larry. "It's no use."

Mr. Stevenson opened the door. "Children, I don't have much left. Will a good ham do?" Sherry let out a loud wail. "What's wrong with your sister?" the butcher asked.

Terry shook his head. "She's just hungry, that's all."

Mr. Stevenson scratched his head. "I've got some T-bone steaks left."

Larry piped up, "Pilgrims didn't celebrate Thanksgiving with T-bones. They ate turkey. We got to have a turkey."

Something dawned on the butcher. "Aha, I've got it!"

"Great!" shouted Terry. "Is it a turkey?"

"Of course. It's the biggest bird I had. Spent three days cookin' it."

"It's already cooked?" asked Larry. "That would be very nice."

Mr. Stevenson puffed out his chest. "It's a thirty-pound smoked turkey. Been three days in the smoker. I was savin' it for myself, but if the Rev. Youngun needs it . . ."

While the butcher wrapped the turkey, Larry whispered to Terry, "I don't know about a smoked turkey."

Terry shook his head. "Pa won't notice the difference, and Four-Eyes won't even be able to see the bird. Pa'll just think that Mrs. Springer did somethin' special to it."

"You sure? Pa will whack us for sure if he catches us lyin'! What if he talks to Mrs. Springer about this?"

Terry laughed. "The chance of that is slim to none. By the time the holiday's over, Pa'll have forgotten all about it."

Mr. Stevenson interrupted them. "Here's your turkey, children. Tell your father I wish him a happy Thanksgiving."

As the Younguns struggled to keep the turkey balanced on the sled-ride home, their father and Four-Eyes Johnson were in the sleigh, on the way home. They stopped at the Willow Creek bridge to let Eulla Mae and Polly pass, because with the snow on the bridge, there was only enough room for one sleigh at a time.

"Hello, Rev. Youngun," Eulla Mae called out. "Happy Thanksgiving, Mr. Johnson."

Four-Eyes wiped the snow from his glasses and peered through the thick lenses. "Who's that?" he mumbled.

Rev. Youngun grinned. "Eulla Mae Springer and her sister Polly. Be polite and wave back."

Four-Eyes began waving in the wrong direction, and the two women giggled.

Rev. Youngun smiled. "Happy Thanksgiving, ladies. Eulla Mae, I can't thank you and Maurice enough for takin' care of our turkey and cookin' it for us. You don't know how much I appreciate it."

From the look of surprise on her face, Rev. Youngun knew that something was up.

Eulla Mae didn't know what he was talking about. "If you're invitin' yourselves to dinner, you know you're more than welcome to eat at our house any time," she said.

Rev. Youngun tipped his hat. "That's very kind of you, but I think someone's cooked his own goose this time."

"Goose?" mumbled Four-Eyes. "I thought we were havin' turkey?" Rev. Youngun tipped his hat and snapped the reins. As they crossed the bridge, Four-Eyes said proudly, "Those are the nicest two blondes I've ever known."

"How long have you known 'em?" Rev. Youngun asked, trying to hold back a laugh.

"Well, I guess I've known Eulla Mae since she was just a baby."

"I guess you've seen a lot in your time," Rev. Youngun said, tongue-in-cheek.

Four-Eyes nodded his head, missing the joke. "Guess I have seen a lot," he said. "Nothin' much escapes me. Just 'cause I wear thick glasses, don't mean I don't know what's goin' on."

As the Rev. Youngun's sleigh whisked across the bridge, Eulla Mae turned to Polly. "First he was talkin' 'bout me cookin' a turkey, then he talks 'bout someone cookin' his own goose. That don't make much sense to me."

Polly sighed. "White folks don't make a whole lot of sense to me, anyway. Especially Mr. Johnson. I've been workin' next door to the hotel for years, and every time he sees me, he tells me he likes the color of my hair."

"What's wrong with that?" Eulla Mae asked, snapping the reins on the horses.

"Nothin', I guess," Polly said, shaking the snow off her curly black hair. " 'Cept that he's nicknamed me Blondie."

CHAPTER 15

BELLS OF GLORY

Rose paced nervously up and down the aisle of the train. First, the engine had broken down near Poplar Bluff; then a frozen steer had to be removed from the tracks outside Fremont. Finally the train came to an abrupt halt just a few miles from Mansfield. The tracks ahead were blocked by a twenty-foot snowdrift! All the engineer could do was wait for help.

A blast of cold wind chilled the car as the conductor entered. He brushed the snow off his cap and put his gloved hands over his unprotected ears.

"How much longer we goin' to be stuck here?" asked a crotchety farmer carrying a wooden crate with two live chickens in it. "I'm gettin' powerful hungry."

The conductor shook his head. "Could be till nightfall, maybe tomorrow morning."

The old farmer stood up. "What are we goin' to eat?"

An old black man, wrapped in a blanket, turned from the seat in front and said, "We could start with them chickens." Almost everyone in the car laughed.

"These are my prize breeding chickens. They're not for eatin'!" the farmer snorted.

The old man pretended to inspect the chickens. "Yup, they each got two drumsticks on 'em. They're prize fryin' chickens, all right!"

Rose followed the conductor out onto the platform. The wind whipped her wool skirt. "Excuse me," she said, tapping him on the shoulder, "but you said we might be stuck here until tomorrow morning. Can't something be done to get us moving? I want to get home for Thanksgiving."

"Young lady, if I could move the snowbank, I would. I want to be with my kids in Springfield for Thanksgivin'. Nobody on this train is happy 'bout this."

Rose looked out at the bleak white landscape. Snow was deep on the ground and getting deeper by the minute. Wind whipped snow flurries around the train, making visibility all but impossible.

"But I wanted to see my mother and father," she said, looking down.

The conductor sighed. "All I can do is keep you informed." He checked the platform's lantern and continued into the next car.

Rose went back to her seat and sat back down. The old man leaned over and asked, "What's wrong, child?"

Looking at the man dressed in patched clothes, Rose felt foolish. "Oh, I just wanted to get home for Thanksgiving."

The old man got up and stretched, folded up his blanket, walked over, and stood beside her. "Just being alive is a Thanksgivin' every day. Yes, sir, when you get older, each sunrise means another day you can find somethin' new before St. Peter calls."

"I know."

"Girl, you have two arms, two legs, and a healthy body. You got somethin' to be thankful for every day."

He leaned over and whispered, "See that poor lamb up

there?" he said, pointing to a crippled boy sitting in his mother's lap. "That boy can't even walk over here to listen to you complain. Yet you're moanin' and worryin' 'bout gettin' home."

Rose knew that whatever she said would ring hollow, following his searing truth. He was right, she acknowledged.

"Where you from?" he asked.

"Mansfield. That's in Wright County."

"I know where it is. Know some folks there."

"You do?" She brightened up. "Where are you from?"

"Seymour. We're practically neighbors. Why, if I was your age, I'd figure a way to get home."

Rose sighed. "Don't see how. We'd need a magic carpet to get over this snowdrift. We need a miracle."

"Shoot, girl, just listen for the bells of glory. They're always ringin' somewhere in your head. Let's try listenin'," he said, cocking his ear toward the snow-covered window.

The silence was broken by the chickens' clucking and two country women talking quietly in the back. Then they heard it at the same time. A bell was jingling. But it wasn't outside; it was from inside the car.

The old man turned at the same time Rose did. The crippled boy was playin' with a bell attached to his mittens, mittens that would never be used to make a snowball, climb a tree, or do anything that was part of a normal, little-boy life.

"The bells of glory," the old man whispered. "I got to hear them one more time."

Then they both heard the jingle bells outside the train. Rose slid over and wiped the fog from the window. Through the smudged clearing, she saw a long cutter with four horses emerging from a swirl of snow.

A red-cheeked, chubby man, with flowing white hair and beard, was sitting on his sleigh. Rose had to blink. "It looks just like Santa Claus," she whispered.

The old man fumbled to find his glasses. "First the bells of

glory, and now Santa Claus. St. Peter must be callin' me for sure!" Closing his eyes, he began humming an old gospel tune to himself.

On the side of the man's sleigh was the symbol of the U.S. Mail. Rose jumped from her seat and went out onto the chilly platform. "Yoo-hoo, Mr. Mailman!" she called, waving her arm.

The white-haired man turned. "Yes?" he asked, putting a red stocking cap onto his head. "What do you want? I'm very busy this time of year."

"Are you going to Mansfield?"

The mailman snorted. "I go lots of places; still I've been wondering why I agreed to this run. But the mail was held up by the snow. Postmaster said we deliver in rain, sleet, and even snow, so I volunteered to get the mail to Mansfield."

"Can I come with you? Please? I want to get home!"

"Where's home?" he asked, checking the reins on the horses.

"Apple Hill Farm, the Wilders'."

"Apple Hill Farm? Think I got a letter from the Cairo port for that place."

"You do?" Rose exclaimed.

"Let's see," he said, reaching into his bag, "I know it's here someplace." Pulling out the letter, he eyed it closely. "Yup, sure do."

Rose reached for it, but he held it above his head. "What's your name?" he asked her, closing one eye.

"Rose Wilder. Can I have the letter, please?"

"That's the name it's addressed to, all right," the mailman said. "But how do I know you're who you say you are?"

"Because I am!" she huffed, stamping her feet. She broke through the snowcrust underfoot and slipped to the ground.

The mailman laughed. "Well, I guess you are who you say you are." He reached over the sleigh and pulled her back up. "Here, Rose Wilder of Apple Hill Farm. Here's your letter."

She took it from his hand. It was from Mary Lou Tibleaux,

and the envelope was marked *Mississippi Queen*. "Will you take me with the letter when you deliver it?"

"I just delivered it. It don't have to go no further."

"But I want to go home."

The chubby mailman turned to leave. Rose jumped from the train into the snow and fell on her face. She stood up as fast as she could and stumbled to the sleigh.

"Please, will you take me as far as Mansfield? I asked for a miracle, and here you are. You've got to take me home!"

"First, brush the snow off your face. You look like a snowman," he grinned.

She brushed the snow off and shook her hair. "Now, will you take me to Mansfield?"

"No, I'll . . ."

Rose interrupted him, "Please, I . . ."

He shook his head. "Why do you young folks always interrupt your elders?"

Rose blushed against the cold. "I'm sorry. I just wanted . . ."

He laughed. "I know what you want. You want to be home with your family like the rest of the world. You never really know how much you miss your parents until they're gone."

"Will you take me, please?"

"I ain't got nothin' better to do than deliver the mail on this holiday. Now that the missus is gone, I just work the holidays to keep my mind off things."

"You'll take me?"

"I got to go to Mansfield anyway, and since there's that letter in your hand addressed to someplace called Apple Hill Farm, why I don't think Uncle Sam would mind if I deliver you at the same time."

Rose heard a tapping on the window from inside the car. The old black man was smiling, and mouthing the words, *Take me too.*

Rose turned to the postman. "So you'll take us?"

"Us? *Me* ain't *us*. I can't be takin' a whole trainful of people along."

"Just the two of us. Please?" she pleaded.

The horses whinnied and snorted, wanting to go. The mailman checked them with the reins. "You better hurry up. Go get your friend, or we're liable to get snowed in right here."

Rose trudged back through the snow and climbed up onto the platform. She stamped her feet, then opened the door. All the passengers turned as the blast of frosty air she let in whipped by them.

Rose grabbed her bag, turned to the old man, and said, "Let's go. He won't wait long."

The old man grabbed his blanket and cloth suitcase. He turned to the farmer and said, "Hope your chickens make it through the night. Lots of hungry people on this train."

The farmer's eyes darted back and forth, calculating who would make the first move to eat his prize chickens. He wrapped his arms around the cage as if he were guarding a treasure.

At the back of the train car, the old man held the door for Laura. Then they heard it again. The boy was jingling his bell.

Rose put down her bag and reached inside it, feeling through the contents. "Here it is," she exclaimed.

"What? What you got?" the old man asked, looking at the small wrapped gift in her hand.

Rose smiled, "I was bringing this antique Bible to my parents . . . I think I'll give it to that little boy."

As Rose walked toward the front, the boy jingled his bell again. The old man said, "Bells of glory, Santa Claus, and now an angel givin' a Bible. Someone pinch me. I surely must be dead now."

The mailman shouted, "Hurry up, you two. We've got to get goin'!"

Rose put the wrapped Bible into the boy's twisted hands and said softly, "You taught me the meaning of Thanksgiving."

The boy's mother looked into her eyes. "He don't understand much." The crippled boy jingled his bell again and weakly smiled up at Rose, making a pitiful sound. His mother said, "I think he said thank you."

Rose flicked the boy's bell with her fingers. "You read this to him. There's a better place for all of us, a place where your son will be able to skip and run with the rest of the angel children."

With his crippled fingers, the boy reached over and cupped her hand. "Thannnnnnnnnnnnnnnnnn Uuuu uuuuuuuuuuuuu," he moaned, smiling up to her.

"No, it's I who should thank you," Rose whispered. Her eyes welled up. "You've taught me to be thankful for what I have. God bless you both."

The mailman shouted again, "I'm leavin' on the count of ten. One, two . . ."

The old man shouted in a cracked voice, "Come on, girl, or we're goin' to be left here with the prize fryin' chickens!"

Rose kissed the crippled boy on the cheek and dashed up the aisle. On the edge of the platform, they heard the mailman, ". . . four, five . . ."

Rose said to the old man, "I don't even know your name."

He stuck out his hand. "Lemuel. Lemuel Springer."

Rose shook his hand. "Pleased to meet you, Mr. Lemuel Springer. My name is Rose, Rose Wilder."

The mailman's voice interrupted them, ". . . six, seven . . ." The horses snorted and whinnied in the air.

"Come on, Miss Wilder. Help me off here. I don't want to break these old bones," Lemuel said.

Rose got down and gave him a hand. "Springer? Are you related to the Springers in Mansfield?"

As they walked toward the sleigh, the old man asked, "The black Springers, or the white Springers?"

"Well, I guess the black Springers. I . . ."

He interrupted her stammering. "That was just a black joke. Yes, I got a second cousin there by the name of Maurice."

Rose interrupted. "They're our neighbors!"

". . . eight, nine . . ."

As they reached the sleigh, the old man muttered, "I'm in heaven, all right. Now I'm meetin' white folks with black folks as friends and neighbors. St. Peter, where are you?"

As they climbed aboard, the mailman cracked his whip. They held on for dear life as the sleigh jolted forward, breaking from the ice crust that had formed underneath the runners.

The sleigh bells jingled with each step as the horses took up a rhythm. The mailman patted the seat next to him and motioned Rose forward. "Let's talk," he said loudly.

Lemuel lay back on the mail sacks and covered himself with his blanket. "Yup," Lemuel mumbled, "this is goin' to heaven in style. Ridin' with Santa Claus himself." Within moments he was fast asleep.

"Well?" the mailman said with a booming voice. "What did it say?"

Rose looked bewildered. "What did what say?"

"Your letter, girl! Don't you know that mailmen are always curious 'bout what they're deliverin'?"

Rose laughed. "What's your name?"

He reached out his gloved hand. "Kris Kringle."

"Kris Kringle? Like the European Santa Claus?"

"Yup," he laughed. "My mother had a good Norwegian sense of humor, and since our last name was Kringle, she named me Kris."

"Did the children rib you?" Rose asked.

"It was never easy around the holidays, until I got older and my hair turned white. Now children and adults are nice to me 'cause they think I look like Santa."

Rose laughed. "You do!"

"Well, I'm glad my last name wasn't Nicholas, 'cause Mother

would have probably named me Saint." He smiled at Rose. "Saint Nicholas would be a bit pretentious, don't you think?"

Rose shrugged. "I don't know. Being named after the Russian patron saint of children wouldn't be all that bad."

"So many names for Santa around the world. Kris Kringle, St. Nicholas. A Mexican man last week shouted out in Spanish, 'Fleece Navidad,' or somethin' like that."

"Feliz Navidad means Merry Christmas in Spanish, I think."

"Si," he laughed, cracking the whip again. He maneuvered the sleigh around a fallen tree. "Well, what did the letter say?"

"I haven't read it yet. You just gave it to me."

"Come on. Read it. Aren't you curious?"

Rose laughed. "Not as curious as you." Rose took the letter out of her pocket and opened it. In a scrawled hand written on *Mississippi Queen* letterhead, Mary Lou Tibleaux had written:

Dear Rose,

I'm sorry that we fussed on the boat. I'm embarrassed to say that I was jealous of what you have and what you were going home to.

I pretended to want to go home to all the parties, but I was sad that my parents didn't care much one way or another if I were home for Thanksgiving. They are always busy with other things like business and charity functions.

Last year, I ate Thanksgiving dinner with the cooks because my parents went to a client's house for dinner. Said I couldn't go along because it was an opportunity for them to make a lot of money.

So beneath this party girl is a pretty lonely person. Your mother's wagon stories are wonderful. I just wish my parents had done something even once with me that could have made one memory that you have.

The only memories I have are of being handed everything but given nothing. Money can't buy love. I

want to be your friend, and didn't want to sadden your
family during the holiday.
Love,
Mary Lou

Rose put down the letter and felt her eyes well up. Kris Kringle saw the first tear ice on her cheek and cracked his whip. "Come on, girl," he shouted into the flurries of snow falling around them. "It's time to be happy! You're goin' home for Thanksgivin'!"

Rose tried to smile. "I'm sorry."

"I'm sorry I had you read that letter."

"I would have had to read it sometime," Rose said, brushing the snow off her hair. "Why were you so eager for me to read the letter?"

"I'm always curious about what I'm deliverin'. Sometimes the letters with perfume on 'em get me so curious that I get a headache wonderin' what they say." He looked over at Rose. "I don't know why I'm tellin' you this."

He cracked his whip and snapped the reins again. Rose waited for him to continue. "I never open anyone's letters, 'cept of course if they open by themselves or get ripped. Then I have to read 'em to find out who they belong to."

Rose smiled. "From the way you talk, it sounds as if you've been to college."

"Thanks, young lady, but the one thing I do is listen a lot. You can learn somethin' every day if you'll just open your ears." He took off his cap. "See this red cap? The other day I learned that penguins can't see the color red. 'Course I don't know how they asked a penguin 'bout that, but that's what the man told me who was readin' the *National Geographic* at the post office."

"Reading someone's mail, eh?" she said in a joking tone.

"Not mail, just a magazine. Postmen get bored, so why not

read a magazine that's sittin' in front of them? Saves two bits on buyin' it!"

Rose laughed. "Tell me another secret."

"Like what?" he asked.

"Do you talk to yourself on these long, lonely trips between towns?"

"Sure! Best person in the world to talk to is yourself, 'cause you always tell yourself exactly what you want to hear!" They both laughed at that.

"You know what else I like to do?" he asked.

"I hope it's not freeze to death," Rose said, pulling her woolen scarf tighter.

"I like to sing. Come on, let's sing. It's the only way I can keep my sanity on these lonely trips." He grabbed the sleigh bells and jingle-jangled in time with a hearty chorus of "Jingle Bells."

Rose joined in as the sleigh's runners flew over the snow. Lemuel turned and cocked his head, "They're singin' 'Jingle Bells.' I must have slept through Thanksgiving." He snuggled back down under his blanket. "Think I'll just sleep till New Year's. That way I'll know I've lived another year."

While Rose was speeding home, joyously singing with Kris Kringle, Laura stood on her porch. She looked through the driving snow, as if expecting to see a miracle.

Manly walked out and put his arm on her shoulder. "Come on in, Laura. She's not goin' to make it home for Thanksgivin' dinner."

"Oh, Manly, I'm just worried that she's all right. When the sheriff told us this morning about the two vagrants he'd found frozen to death outside town, I got so scared."

"Rose is your daughter, Laura. She knows how to take care of herself."

Laura shook her head. "But she's only a young girl."

Manly smiled. "She's a woman now, goin' on eighteen, and

she has your gift of gab. Wherever she is, you can bet she's talkin' her way into or out of something."

"Oh, Manly, she's not . . ."

"Not, poppycock!" he interrupted. "She's all right. Probably just snowed in at some fancy hotel with that high-falutin' friend of hers, orderin' a fancy meal." He turned back toward the doorway. "And speakin' of food, let's go see if the turkey's ready. I'm starvin'!"

Just a few miles away, Rose was chewing happily on a piece of turkey jerky. "Made it myself," said Kris. "Ain't fancy, but it'll keep you alive."

Rose stuffed another peppery piece into her mouth. "Best meal I've had since the wagon trip from the Dakotas."

"What? Couldn't hear ya."

"This is the best Thanksgiving turkey I've ever had," she said, chewing on the stringy piece of turkey jerky.

CHAPTER 16

SMOKED TURKEY

Rev. Youngun decided not to let on that he'd talked with Eulla Mae Springer. Though he'd never admit it to his children, he was amused at their ingenuity. They'd gone to a lot of trouble to save Teddy Roosevelt's neck, so at least he could delay the inevitable until after the meal. Besides, he was interested in seeing how they'd work the whole thing out.

The butcher had included some special giblet dressing that he'd made up for another customer, so all the Younguns really had to do was heat everything up. There were leftover mashed potatoes that some of the church ladies had brought over and a tureen of potato soup from Mrs. Peterson, the sheriff's wife. With the jars of peaches and pears in the root cellar, they had a pretty good meal.

Larry didn't say much, because lying always made him feel bad. Sherry kept quiet because she was just glad they weren't about to eat Teddy Roosevelt. But Terry couldn't leave well enough alone. He just had to add on to the story, telling whopper after whopper.

"Pa," Terry smiled, nodding his head, "that Mrs. Springer is a wonderful cook." He pointed to the smoked turkey on the table. "Who'd have thought that ol' Teddy Roosevelt would cook up like that in one afternoon?"

"It is hard to believe, isn't it?" said Rev. Youngun, shaking his head at the audacity of his son. "Larry, what do you have to say about all this?"

Under the gaze of his father, Larry began to wilt. He didn't want to compound the lie, but he didn't know what else to do. It was kind of like sneaking into a neighbor's yard when you shouldn't be there, then turning around and finding a snarling dog blocking the way out. The only choice was to continue toward the other side of the yard, hoping you'd get out alive.

"Well, Pa," Larry stammered, "I think the turkey came out all right."

"It's got an unusual color and texture to it, don't you think?" Rev. Youngun asked.

"What color is it? Ain't spoiled, is it?" Four-Eyes Johnson asked.

The kids began snickering, and Rev. Youngun noticed that Sherry and Terry were moving Four-Eyes' silverware around. "Stop that," he whispered.

"Stop what?" Four-Eyes asked. "Can we eat yet?"

"First, let's say grace," Rev. Youngun said.

"Would you mind if I took out my teeth for a moment?" Four-Eyes asked. "They're hurtin' real bad."

Rev. Youngun didn't know what to say. "Well, I . . . they're your teeth and . . ."

Four-Eyes wiggled his fingers around in his mouth and pulled out his chompers. The Younguns were transfixed, silently watching Four-Eyes place his teeth on the napkin next to his plate. Terry and Sherry bumped heads, leaning over to look at them.

The only problem was, without his teeth in, he couldn't pronounce his c's and s's. "That'th muth better."

"Why can't you speak good?" Sherry asked, staring up at the toothless man sitting next to her.

" 'Thauth without my teeth, it'th hard to thpeak."

"They made from wood?" Terry asked.

Four-Eyes licked his gums and moved his jaw back and forth. "No, thur, they're made from whale tuthkth," he said, really trying to pronounce the words.

"Tuthkth?" Sherry asked, "what's a tuthkth?"

Rev. Youngun rolled his eyes. "Whale tusks, that's what Mr. Johnson said."

Terry looked at the teeth. "I still don't understand why you talk funny without your clackers in, Mr. Johnson. Can your clackers talk by themselves?"

Four-Eyes turned to answer Terry, but he talked to the coat rack instead. " 'Cuth I juth do and no, my thlathkerth than't tal by themthelveth."

"Who would like to say grace?" Rev. Youngun asked.

Sherry shot up her hand, and let out a burp my mistake, " 'Scuse me," then remembered why she'd put up her hand. "I want to. My turn!"

"No," Rev. Youngun said, "I think that on this special occasion, when our neighbors did us such a kindness, we should let . . ." He paused, looking at Terry and Larry. Both of them slipped down in their chairs.

". . . let Terry say the blessing. Son, will you do us the honor?"

Terry looked down and ran his words together, "DoIhavetosayit, Pa?"

"Son, I'm sure you'll do a fine job."

Terry gulped, "Lord . . . ah . . . thank you for the smo . . ." He stopped himself from saying smoked turkey. "Ah, thank you for the smoldering, hot turkey that Mrs. Springer made for us hungry children, who miss their momma and just wanted to make Pa's day easier. The food will taste good 'cause . . ." he paused and eyed his father, whose head was bowed, ". . . 'cause I've already had a few nibbles. And thank you for bringing Four-E . . ."

His father's head shot up, mouthing the word *no*. Terry caught himself. "And, ah, . . . thank you for having Mr. Johnson share this meal and let us look at his clacker teeth. I love you, Lord. Oh yeah, remember that when you're lookin' down on me for other things you may be thinkin'. Amen."

Rev. Youngun unfolded his napkin. "That was very good, Terry. I'm sure that we all need a little extra understandin' for the things we get ourselves into, now, don't we?" He was giving his children every opportunity to confess, but none of them were biting at the chance.

"Than I thay grath?" Mr. Johnson asked.

Rev. Youngun couldn't turn his guest down. "Certainly, Mr. Johnson. We'd be delighted."

Rev. Youngun didn't notice what his children were doing. Terry looked at Larry, who shook his head no. Terry nodded his head yes and carefully picked up Four-Eyes' teeth.

While everyone bowed their heads, Terry held the teeth up behind Four-Eyes. As Four-Eyes began to say his blessing, Terry mimicked him by moving the teeth as if they were talking.

Four-Eyes bowed his head and said, "Than you tho muthh for the blething we are about to rethieve." Terry was playing merrily with the teeth behind his head. "Thith ith a thpethial othathion on Thankthgiving and we thintheerly thank you for tho muthh that you have blethed uth with."

Terry was still playing away with the teeth behind Four-Eyes' head when his father looked up. Terry quickly put the teeth back on the napkin.

Rev. Youngun shook his head in disappointment. "Terry, what do you have to say about the special blessing Mr. Johnson just gave?"

Terry patted Four-Eyes on the back. "Thoudth thpethial to me!" Larry put his napkin in front of his face to hide his smile, and even Rev. Youngun had to turn away so Terry wouldn't see his grin.

With the sharp carving knife, Rev. Youngun sliced a stack of breast meat while the kids slurped their soup. They sounded like three drains sucking down the last bit of bathtub water.

Rev. Youngun looked up. "Children, please stop that." A long, loud slurp answered him.

"Thorry," Four-Eyes said sheepishly, putting his teeth back in. He moved them back and forth until they felt right. "Sorry. You kind of forget manners when you eat by yourself all the time."

"We're just glad you could join us," Rev. Youngun said.

Four-Eyes smiled and showed his gums. "Sure do appreciate your havin' me to dinner."

The plates were passed for turkey, and the side dishes circled the table. "More rolls, Mr. Johnson?" Larry asked.

Four-Eyes adjusted his glasses and looked down. "Huh? I just took two? Now what'd I do with 'em? Eat 'em?" He took two more which Terry and Sherry quickly grabbed when he turned his back.

Rev. Youngun began slicing a drumstick for seconds and noticed a tag hanging on it. "What's this?" he asked. "Why, it says, Stevenson's Butcher Shop. How'd that get there?"

Larry wanted to get it over with. "Pa, I want to tell you . . ."

Terry, who didn't want to get a wuppin', interrupted him. "Pa, what he wants to tell you is that that tag was on ol' Teddy Roosevelt since the day he was a baby gobbler. Yes-sir-re-bob, that's where the church lady got the baby turkey. From Stevenson's Butcher Shop and Baby Turkey Farm."

Rev. Youngun kept a straight face. "I didn't know they tagged every baby turkey."

Larry sank down in his seat until his forehead was practically touching the table. Sherry sat transfixed, absorbing another dose of misinformation from her squirrelly brother.

Terry puffed up like a politician on a roll. *"You didn't know that?* They always tag turkey feet at birth, so the momma turkeys can tell their little gobblers apart. Just like in the St. Louis hospital when you took us there to see Sherry, who looked like a wet rat."

"Did not!" Sherry screamed.

Rev. Youngun raised his voice. "Children. Children, stop it!" He stared them into silence. "I was just trying to figure out how the tag got on the drumstick." He looked directly at Terry. "So Teddy Roosevelt had this on him all the time, huh?" He looked again at the tag. "Why, it says thirty pounds—two dollars. That's a mighty big baby turkey."

Larry's head hit the table, but Terry was undaunted. "Yup, turkey doctor said he was the biggest turkey ever born in Wright County. When he was born they called him Goliath, but we named him Teddy Roosevelt."

"How about that?" said Rev. Youngun. "Wish I could see Teddy Roosevelt one more time," he sighed.

Rev. Youngun looked at the tag again. "Hm. It says 'smoked for three days.' Wonder what that means?"

Terry didn't miss a beat. "That's what I was tellin' you, but you didn't let me finish. Durn near took three days for his birthin'. It was so hard they called it a smokin' birth. Every turkey tag has to list how long the birthin' was; that's the law."

"Is that a fact?" Rev. Youngun said.

"The fact's on the table," Terry said, pointing to the turkey. "There lies a good, good bird. T.R. was a good pet. I'll miss him." Terry bowed his head and mouthed a short, silent prayer.

Rev. Youngun shook his head in false sympathy. "Wish I could see Teddy Roosevelt just one more time."

"He's right in front of you, Pa," Terry exclaimed.

"No, I mean, just see him in the yard and hear him gobble one more time."

Sherry gulped. "You want to see him right now, Pa?"

Terry kicked her under the table. "Pa, you're goin' to get her upset, thinkin' 'bout it. I don't think I'll ever forget how that brave bird looked over at us as the axe was fallin'. I could almost hear him sayin' his last words, which sounded like . . ."

"Gobble-gobble." Teddy Roosevelt, in the flesh, stood at the doorway, with Terry's stocking cap stuck on his head.

Four-Eyes Johnson looked over and said to Rev. Youngun, "Thought you only had three children."

"Gobble-gobble." Teddy Roosevelt came up and stood next to the table.

Rev. Youngun's face grew stern. "I want the truth now, children. I saw Mrs. Springer today, and she invited us to eat at her house. Didn't know a thing 'bout cookin' us a turkey."

Teddy Roosevelt pecked a roll out of Four-Eyes' hand, who grabbed it right back. "Rev. Youngun," Four-Eyes exclaimed, "you need to teach this sorry-lookin' child of yours some manners."

Wiping off his glasses with his napkin, Four-Eyes peered at the turkey. Teddy Roosevelt shook his head back and forth, flapping his long, red gobble sack. Four-Eyes shook his head. "Poor child. Ain't never seen a child with a case of gout that bad. He sure is pitiful lookin'."

Rev. Youngun sat and stared. The silence was deafening. Terry wanted to faint.

"Well?" Rev. Youngun asked.

"Pa," Larry said, clearing his throat, "I want to tell you that no one cut off Teddy Roosevelt's head."

The turkey gobble-gobbled and ambled up next to Rev. Youngun. "I think that's obvious. Go on."

"Well, Pa, it was like this." Larry told the truth, the whole truth, and nothing but the truth, beginning with the bobcat eating the turkey in the turkey tree, to getting the smoked turkey from the butcher. "And we used all our money we'd saved to buy the turkey for you, Pa."

Rev. Youngun sighed and settled down into his chair. Four-

Eyes Johnson took his teeth out again and laid them on a napkin, then fell fast asleep at the table.

Sherry picked up the teeth and began clacking them at Larry, but a stern look from her father stopped her. She put the teeth back on the napkin while Four-Eyes Johnson snored away, oblivious to it all.

Terry felt bad but he took the opportunity to carefully turn the back side of the turkey toward him. When his father wasn't looking, he clamped Four-Eyes' teeth onto the turkey's rear end.

Rev. Youngun started to speak but noticed the false teeth biting down on the turkey's diamond-shaped behind. "Can't you let up for just a moment, Terry? For goodness sake, when is enough enough?"

Terry looked down. "Sorry, Pa. Just tryin' to get a laugh."

Terry lifted the teeth off the turkey's tail end and placed them back on Four-Eyes' napkin. The old man snored away, still unaware of a thing.

Rev. Youngun looked at his children and said quietly, "Lying is bad. I've told you that. I've made you write 'I shall not lie' on paper, I've stood you in the corner, and I've paddled each of you." He paused, looking into their eyes. "I used to believe that if you spared the rod you spoiled the child. But you children are different. I love you, but if I can't trust you, then my job becomes nothin' more than bein' a guardian until you're ready to move out on your own."

"We don't want to leave," Sherry whimpered. "I want to live here forever."

"All children feel that way until they grow into the person they're goin' to be. All I'm tryin' to do is help make sure that the person you grow into is a good person. Good people tell the truth."

Rev. Youngun took Terry's hand and looked into his eyes. "Lying begins at a very early age . . . about Sherry's age," he said, looking over at her. "But little liars can't hide their guilty feelings very well, so parents pick up on their guilt signs." She looked down. "By about your age, Terry, if lyin' habits haven't been stopped, a child starts gettin' pretty good at it."

"I'm sorry, Pa," Terry said with downcast eyes.

"Me too," said Larry.

"I know you both are now, but that's because you got caught. You children have very vivid imaginations, which is great, but there's a difference between fantasy and lyin'. When you were make-believe marchin' to battle with Teddy Roosevelt on a leash, well, that was fantasy, and that's okay."

He took a sip of milk and used the napkin to dab at his lips. The only sound was Four-Eyes' snoring.

Rev. Youngun smiled. "I know that you wanted to save Teddy Roosevelt, and you came up with a great idea to buy the smoked turkey with your own money. If you'd just come to me with the plan, I would have agreed to it. But you didn't. You concocted a plan built on fibs and deception."

He paused, wringing his hands for effect. The children watched, hoping that they weren't going to get a spanking. "Let me tell you the story about a boy named Pinocchio and what happened to him when he told a lie."

As Rev. Youngun began the children's story, Terry hung on every word. He was bothered so much that he kept feeling his nose every few moments, to see if it had grown. Teddy Roosevelt listened from the hallway with his head cocked.

After they'd cleared the table and cleaned the dishes, the Younguns said good night to their father. "Say good night to Mr. Johnson, if he's awake," their father said.

Four-Eyes snored away, so Larry walked quietly by. Terry started to take his glasses, but Larry grabbed his arm. "Don't! Pa's mad enough as it is."

Larry pulled Terry from the room, his hand over Terry's mouth. Sherry walked up, peeked up at Four-Eyes, then looked at his teeth and picked them up. "Good night, Mr. Johnson," she said to his teeth. She clacked the teeth, saying, out of the side of her mouth, "Good night," then followed her brothers.

After the children left the room, Teddy Roosevelt walked back in and pulled the teeth off Four-Eyes' napkin. He put them on the floor and tried to peck the food from them, then picked them up again with his beak and gobbled and wobbled out of the dining room. T.R. dropped them into the hood of Terry's coat and went and stood near the warm fire in the parlor.

Four-Eyes awakened and looked around through his thick glasses, trying to remember where he was. He flapped his gums up and down, wiggled his jaw back and forth, and felt the napkin for his teeth.

Rev. Youngun came in from the kitchen. "Come on, Mr. Johnson. I'll fix up the couch for you to sleep on."

Four-Eyes waved his arms around as he stood up. "My teeth. Have you theen my teeth?"

Rev. Youngun shook his head. "I'm sure they're here someplace. We'll find 'em in the morning."

After he'd put sheets on the sofa with a warm quilt on top, Rev. Youngun said good night and left the parlor. Four-Eyes snuggled down. With his glasses off, the embers from the fire cast a dancing light throughout the room.

He heard a noise from behind and looked around. "Thay, do you know where my teeth ith?" he asked in the darkened room.

T.R. looked in. "Gobble-gobble?"

CHAPTER 17

APPLE HILL THANKSGIVING

Cubby and Dr. George were invited to Thanksgiving dinner at the Springers', where Polly surprised Dr. George with her wit and charm. Everyone was in a wonderful holiday mood. But across the ravine and down the creek, Apple Hill Farm was filled with gloom.

Laura had held dinner up to the point where the turkey was almost overcooked. She kept hoping against hope that Rose would somehow make it home for Thanksgiving dinner. Finally Laura could wait no longer and served the dinner.

"Manly, why don't you say the blessing?" Laura asked, breaking the silence of the room.

Manly nodded and said a very short, warm prayer for the safety of Rose. It was their first Thanksgiving without Rose since she was born. Every parent faces this at some point, but they had been expecting Rose. The deepening snow, the reports of frozen cattle, dead vagrants, blocked rail lines and roads, cast gloom over the room.

Manly tried to break the mood. "Laura, pass me some more mashed 'taters." He looked at the turkey. "Shame to have this big bird for just you and me. 'Course the bird probably wishes we'd eaten his cousin or a goose or somethin'."

Laura smiled, then grew serious. "Oh, Manly, I'm just so worried. Do you think she's all right?"

"No matter what I say, it all gets down to that I just don't know. There's nothing we can do, Laura."

At that moment, Kris Kringle's sleigh was crossing Willow Creek Bridge. He pulled to a stop and looked at Rose. "Which way, Rosie?"

"It's just up this road." She pointed the way. "Apple Hill is only a mile away."

"Think they've waited dinner for you?" he asked, letting the horses stamp their legs.

"Dinner for *us,* you mean?" Lemuel Springer asked from the rear.

Rose looked back. Lemuel was covered with snow. Only his eyes peered out from under the blanket. "Glad you could join us!" she laughed.

Lemuel stretched his arms. "I need my sleep. When you're old, it ain't no fun. No sir, old age ain't for sissies."

"My mother always makes a big, big Thanksgiving dinner. I'm sure there's enough for all of us."

While the horses snorted and stamped, Lemuel looked around. "Hey, Santa, what you waitin' for?"

Kris Kringle looked at Rose with an embarrassed look. "Never done this before."

"What?" Rose asked.

"Never delivered the person who I was delivering the letter to and then had dinner with them. Might be somethin' in Uncle Sam's regulation book against this."

"What's it say 'bout starvin'?" Lemuel asked.

"What?" Kris asked, looking back.

"These old skin and bones need food, Santa. Crack that whip and let's get on to Rose's home."

Lemuel shook his head, dropping a flurry of snow. "As long as it's not a work farm or the farm behind heaven's gate, I'm ready to go and eat."

Kris cracked his whip, jangled the sleigh bells, and shouted, "Let's sing for our supper!" They headed up the road to Apple Hill Farm, laughing and singing "Jingle Bells."

Laura passed the stewed tomatoes to Manly and cocked her head. "Manly, do you hear something?"

Manly put down the bowl of stewed tomatoes and listened. "Why, it sounds like someone's singin'." He listened again. "It sounds like they're singin' 'Jingle Bells.'"

The sound of the song got louder and louder as the sleigh drew closer. Laura stood up. "Manly, do you think . . . ?"

"Don't know. Maybe it's a church group or somethin'."

The sound of horses snorting and footsteps on the porch stairs gave them the hope they needed. Both of them rushed to the front door as Rose burst through it.

Snow was flying around her head as she hugged her mother. "Oh, Mother, I'm home! I made it home for Thanksgiving!"

Manly stood behind them. "Glory be, girl, we thought it was Santa himself comin'."

"Did somebody call me?" Kris Kringle asked, standing in the doorway with his full white beard, long white hair, and red stocking cap.

Manly stepped back. "Well, I'll be. I must be seeing things."

"Mother and Dad, this is Kris Kringle, the mailman who delivered me home for Thanksgiving."

Laura smiled and shook his hand. "We can't thank you enough."

Kris smiled and winked. "Just call it a special delivery."

Lemuel Springer slid inside the house next to Kris. "And this is me, Lemuel Springer, and my bones are old and cold."

"This is Maurice's cousin," Rose said. "He lives over in Seymour and helped me on the train."

Manly stepped forward. "We're all goin' to freeze to death if we don't close this door."

"Is anybody hungry?" Laura asked. "We just sat down to eat."

"That's why we came," Lemuel said. "Came all this way with Santa to have Thanksgivin' dinner at Apple Hill Farm."

Manly took the two men into the dining room, but Rose stopped her mother in the entranceway. "Mother, I had a gift for you both, but I gave it to someone else."

"Oh?" said Laura, who remembered her daughter as a little girl, always wanting to help others.

"There was a little crippled boy on the train who could barely talk. He was dingling a little bell on his mittens. Lemuel said it sounded like the bells of glory." Rose looked down, then up with a tear in her eye. "You'd have liked it but . . ."

Laura hugged her daughter. "That little boy is one of the angels. You did the right thing."

It was a wonderful Thanksgiving dinner, filled with stories and laughter. Apple Hill Farm seemed to have a glow of happiness as the snow continued to fall.

The meal was testimony that Thanksgiving is a true pilgrim's celebration and gathering. This holiday had brought together a family and two lonely people who had given their hearts to a weary stranger on the road.

In her diary, Laura wrote:

We are inclined to think of Thanksgiving Day as a strictly American institution. But a harvest feast with the giving of praise and thanks is a custom much older than our Thanksgiving that has been, and still is, observed by most races and peoples.

It seems instinctive for the human race to give thanks for benefits bestowed by someone greater than ourselves. But even more than for material blessings, let us, with humble hearts, give thanks for our understanding of the greatness and goodness of God. For only he could have brought Kris Kringle to Rose's train and delivered her home to us.

CHAPTER 18

TERRYOCCHIO?

That evening, alone in his bed, Terry pondered the story of Pinocchio that his father had told him. He'd been feeling his nose all night, to see if it had grown.

This was the first time that his pa hadn't just yelled or paddled him, and it made him feel even worse. At least with a whuppin', he could know it was over and not think about it. Now, he was lying in bed, tossing and turning, worrying about his nose.

Yes, he had told a lie, but don't all kids do that? Larry and Sherry had joined the plan to save Teddy Roosevelt, but they were sleeping peacefully.

Teddy Roosevelt came up and pecked at the covers. "Leave me alone, Teddy. You got me into enough trouble already!"

"Gobble-gobble, gobble-gobble." T.R. pecked at the covers.

"Well, you're lucky we didn't gobble you up for dinner. Tomorrow it's back to the barn for you, turkey."

The turkey gobbled away as Terry fell into a restless sleep. He began dreaming about the story of Pinocchio, but it was all

jumbled up. Terry knew he was dreaming and tried to wake up, but couldn't.

He felt his joints stiffen and looked at his arms. They were wood, with pegged joints. He was a wooden puppet, floating above his house, looking down!

Inside, he could see his father, leaning over the dining room table, talking to Dangit the dog. "Oh, how I wish I had a little boy who would tell the truth. It would be wonderful, wouldn't it, Dangit?"

Dangit asked, "Why don't you wish on the stars and the moon? You are Geppetto Youngun, the best wisher in Missouri!"

Terry was startled. Dangit was talking. "Pa, I'm up here! Come get me, Pa! I want to be your good little boy!" But his father couldn't hear him.

"Oh, dangit!" Terry said, snapping his fingers. "Why can't you hear me?"

Dangit heard somebody misuse his name and raced around the room, barking.

"What's wrong?" asked Geppetto Youngun. "Did someone call your name or misuse it?"

Dangit turned to Geppetto Youngun. "I thought I heard someone misuse my name. You know how upset that makes me."

"Oh, well, you were probably hearin' things."

Terry waved his arms. "No, he wasn't, Pa. I said it! Me, your son Terry, I said it!" But they couldn't hear a word.

Geppetto Youngun looked up toward the heavens. "Oh, how I wish I had a good boy with me right now!"

Terry felt a tap on his shoulder. It was his sister, Sherry, flying around, dressed in fairy clothes with a magic wand in her hand. Terry reached out, but he couldn't grab her. "Hey, Sherry, are you in this dream, too?"

"My name is Sherry the Good Fairy, and Geppetto Youngun

wishes for a good little boy. I'd send him Larry, but I can't seem to find him."

"What about me? I'm good!"

Sherry the Good Fairy flew a circle around him, laughing. "Geppetto Youngun wants a boy who will tell the truth. That's not you."

"I can try. I'll try to tell the truth. My name is Terry and . . ."

"See? You just told a lie," Sherry the Good Fairy said, flying a figure eight in the air.

"I did not! My name is Terry!"

"Liar! Your name is Terryocchio."

"Terryocchio? That sounds like a wooden puppet."

"Look at your arms," she said. "Look at your legs. I wouldn't get too close to a fire, if I were you."

Terryocchio tapped his arms and legs. "How'd this happen?"

"In dreams, anythin' can happen," Sherry the Good Fairy said. "Now, you're goin' to make Geppetto Youngun's dream come true."

Before he could respond, she whacked him hard on the head with her magic wand and watched him float down through the roof into the house. "I wanted to do that for a long time," she said, flying off.

Geppetto Youngun, blinded by a flash of brilliant light, rubbed his eyes. As the dazzling display disappeared, he blinked again. "Who are you?" he asked.

Terryocchio blinked and rubbed his wooden eyes. "Pa, my name is Terryocchio, and I'm your new son!"

Geppetto Youngun grabbed Terryocchio and danced around the room with him. "My new son! My truth-tellin' new son!" He set Terryocchio down. "You must be hungry. All little boys are. Do you want to have Thanksgivin' dinner with me?"

"Don't trust him. He tells fibs," said Dangit.

"Please, Pa," pleaded Terryocchio. "I won't. I promise."

"That's my good boy," he said, patting his wooden head.

"Pa, I don't know how I got like this, but . . ."

"But you are hungry, and that's all that matters," said Geppetto Youngun. "Now, what should we have for Thanksgivin' dinner? How 'bout a turkey?"

"Okay, Pa. Whatever you say."

"Good," said Geppetto Youngun. He reached into the cabinet and brought out a tall, sharp axe. "Take this axe and go chop the head off Teddy Roosevelt and bring him back to me."

"Oh, Pa. I can't."

"If you're a good boy, you will do it," he exclaimed, handing Terryocchio the axe.

He pushed Terryocchio out the door along with Dangit and waved after them, "You're my good boy and will do exactly as I say, won't you?"

Terryocchio looked down at Dangit as the door closed. "What are you comin' along for? You hungry or somethin'?"

"No," said Dangit, "I just want to keep an eye on you."

Terryocchio was caught in the same dilemma again. Should he kill Teddy Roosevelt, or tell another fib? He made up his mind that this was just a silly dream and marched past the barn. Terryocchio had made up his mind to go back to the butcher.

"What are you goin' to do?" Dangit yipped.

"I don't know," Terryocchio fibbed, and then caught himself, putting his hand over his nose. That was not true! He looked down and saw his nose sticking through his fingers!

"Liar, liar, pants on fire," Dangit yipped, running in circles.

"Okay, I'm goin' to the butcher. I'm not goin' to kill Teddy Roosevelt." That was the truth, so his nose stopped growing. They walked through the snow into Mansfield and stopped in front of the butcher shop.

"What's wrong?" Dangit asked.

"Name's different," he said, looking at the sign. "Stromboli Stevenson's Butcher Shop."

"Been this way as long as you've been dreamin'," Dangit yipped.

Terryocchio opened the door carefully. At the back of the shop, Stromboli Stevenson was holding Teddy Roosevelt by the neck. "You want me to kill Teddy Roosevelt for your father?" he boomed out.

Terryocchio jumped back. "Yes, er . . . no." He looked down again, and his nose was going in and out, getting longer and shorter.

"What's my nose doing?" he asked Dangit.

"It can't figure out if you're tellin' the truth or not. You answered yes and no to one question."

Stromboli Stevenson boomed out again, "Do you want me to kill this turkey for your father, like he asked you to do? You came here for a turkey, and this is the only one in town. What will it be? Are you going to be a good boy or a bad boy?"

Terryocchio walked forward on his creaky, wooden legs. His nose was going in and out. What was he to do? His father wanted a turkey; he wanted Teddy Roosevelt's head cut off. But Terry didn't.

"Well, boy?" Stromboli Stevenson yelled.

Terryocchio looked up at Teddy Roosevelt, who gobbled to him. "I don't want you to kill Teddy Roosevelt." Suddenly, his nose stopped going in and out.

"Well, boy," Stromboli Stevenson said, "what are you goin' to tell your pa? You want a smoked turkey to trick him with?" Stromboli's laugh shook the room.

"No, dangit!" yelled Terryocchio. "I'm goin' to march home and tell Pa the truth. Then I'll come and buy your ol' smoked turkey!"

Dangit rushed out to grab his pants leg for using his name, but Terryocchio kicked him away. "You bite this wooden leg and you'll get splinters in your mouth, you dummy!"

Terryocchio marched home and told Geppetto Youngun the truth. When he finished, his nose began shrinking, and he cried out, "Look, Pa, I told the truth. I told the truth."

From somewhere beyond the realm of sleep, he felt the calm, reassuring touch of his pa's hands. "Terry. Terry, you're havin' a bad dream. It's all right."

Terry sat up, rubbing his eyes. He carefully touched his nose. It was normal! "Pa, my nose shrank! It's not long anymore . . . I . . ."

"It was just a bad dream," Rev. Youngun said soothingly.

"No, Pa, it was a good dream! I told you the truth." He reached out and hugged his father. "I love you, Pa. I do."

Rev. Youngun sat on the bed with his arms around his little auburn-haired troublemaker. So much mischief but so much potential. *That's what parents are for,* he thought to himself, *to guide these talents toward a fulfilling life.* It was never easy, but it was a job that had to be done for the sake of generations to come.

"I love you, too, Terry," he said, ruffling his son's auburn hair. After a few moments he stood up. "You get some sleep. I'm takin' Teddy Roosevelt out to the barn."

"Don't kill him, Pa. Please," Terry pleaded.

"No, I'm not going to kill him. He belongs in the barn." He picked up Teddy Roosevelt and carried him from the room.

"Good night, Pa." Terry said into the dark.

" 'Night, son," his father answered from the darkened hallway.

"Good night, Teddy Roosevelt," Terry whispered to himself.

"Gobble-gobble, gobble-gobble," Teddy Roosevelt answered from somewhere downstairs.

"You're welcome," Terry whispered, drifting off to sleep.

CHAPTER 19

COLD AND GETTING COLDER

The temperature hovered at or below zero for days on end. The newspaper headlined:

A GREAT CROP OF FROSTBITTEN EARS AND NOSES IS READY TO BE PULLED!

Mansfield, Missouri—December 5, 1905—Jack Frost has hit Missouri with a vengeance, knocking out roads, rails, and communications. Reports of twenty-foot snowdrifts blocking the lines are filtering in from Little Rock and St. Louis.

In Mountain Grove, Missouri, cut off from all provisions, a food riot broke out as the last sack of flour was sold for $40. Cattle rustling has been reported in the outlying areas, with the Wright County sheriff taking on added deputies to cope with the emergency. A report of two cattle rustlers being lynched in Hoxie, Mo., has not been confirmed as we go to press.

A trainload of Polish immigrants heading to Nebraska was stoned as it passed through Sikeston, Missouri, when it wouldn't unload the food provisions bound for Nebraska. A caravan of Missouri Mormons pulling hand carts toward Utah got snowed in outside of Wichita,

Kansas. Ten Mormon men and their thirty-six wives and fifty-eight children perished in the snow.

The governor has asked that we all pray for better weather and that we work together. He put the state militia on alert after riots broke out in St. Louis when a meat truck was overturned in a poor neighborhood.

The people of Mansfield handled the cold and snow as best they could. Those who went outside did their business quickly and then retreated to sit by cookstoves and fireplaces. Bundled townspeople walked as fast as they could on the icy streets, trailing behind them puffs of frozen breath.

It was cold and getting colder. Sunrise meant only a small respite from the biting freeze that followed dusk with a vengeance. December was fulfilling the predictions of a hard winter.

As the snow continued to pile up, Manly sheltered the animals in the barns and used his axe to keep the water troughs open. Even with the wall holes plugged and blankets on the horses and cows, he couldn't protect them all.

A calf slipped out of the barn, and Manly found him frozen straight up against the fence. One of the barn cats got stuck on the roof and almost looked like a weather vane, frozen in place.

Two barns burned down south of town. Though the newspaper ran warnings about leaving stoves and heaters on in hay-stocked barns, the advice was ignored. All it took was a kick from a cow or a bump from a horse to set off a blazing inferno.

Everyone tried to keep cheerful, helping one another, as good neighbors should. A dozen of the elderly from the hills were living in the parish halls of the town's three churches, and a food drive had produced enough donated items to feed the families whose supplies had run out.

Laura had seen the same situation years before in the Dakotas, when a blizzard isolated her town. She could see the strain behind the smiles on the faces of the people of Mansfield.

Though everyone was willing to share what they had to a point, signs of hoarding were appearing.

With food stocks scarce and supplies not getting through, Lafayette Bedal, owner of Bedal's General Store, posted a limit on the number of bags of rice and beans that one person could buy at a time.

A feeling of isolation began to set in as the snow piled deeper and deeper. Snowstorms came up so quickly that anyone venturing too far from their homes risked death. The blizzard conditions were so bad that it was impossible to see your hand in front of your face during the storms. Schools were closed and church attendance dropped off dramatically, as travel became all but impossible.

Two hunters were trapped by a very fierce storm and survived only by gutting their horses and crawling inside the carcasses. One of them lost two fingers to frostbite.

Three more people were found frozen on their farms. Two children who got lost bringing their cows in were found dead inside a shed they'd entered for protection from one of the sudden storms.

A train full of provisions from St. Louis—one that the town had been expecting—was not able to get through, sending shock waves through the community. People realized that they had to make do with what they had in their food bins.

Rev. Youngun, Father Walsh, and Sheriff Peterson organized food deliveries to the outlying areas and reported several families near starvation. Wood supplies were getting low, and entire families moved into the church halls for warmth and food.

Even though business was booming at the hotel, Four-Eyes had not found his teeth yet. He spent his time limping around, looking for them, and refused to order another set.

Lemuel Springer decided to make an extended visit with his cousins, Maurice and Eulla Mae, and Kris Kringle left to finish his mail route, promising to be back before Christmas. He told

Rose, "You've invited me to visit over Christmas, so I might just take you up on it."

Laura spoke at a gathering of the town people on the necessity of sharing their stored provisions, but it seemed that most people only gave the idea lip service.

After her speech, Edwin Ebenezer, a crotchety old veteran, told her, "The Lord helps those who help themselves. Better some live than we all starve."

Cold emotions matched the temperature, which was cold and getting colder.

CHAPTER 20

MEAL FOR TWO

Dr. George sat, deep in thought, in the front room of his house, which served as his office. The tinkling bell over the door rang as a blast of freezing air swept through the house. Without looking up, he turned in his chair. "Can I help . . ." He stopped. It was Polly.

"Dr. George, I hate to bother you."

"No bother at all, Polly. I was just sitting here thinking about how much I missed the hot, sunny days I was cursing just a few months ago."

Polly smiled. "We all miss somethin' later that we didn't 'preciate at the time."

They looked at each other in awkward silence. For the first time, he noticed the beauty of her smile and the hint of humor in her eyes. He broke the silence. "It's a cold day to be out, Polly. What can I do for you?"

She shook the snow off her head. "It's Mr. Johnson! He slipped and sprained his ankle looking for his teeth. Can you come and take a look at it?"

"Looking for his teeth? What happened?" He couldn't help but laugh.

Polly chuckled. "He thought he might have left his teeth in his room on the second floor. But he mistook the cellar stairs for those goin' up and took himself a bad fall."

Dr. George had to grin. "You sure he don't need an eye doctor?"

"If his glasses were any thicker, he'd need a rope to hold them up," she laughed. "Can you come now?"

"Sure. Give me a moment to get my coat and bag," he said, going into the back room. "Doesn't he have a second set of falsies?"

Polly replied, "Had just one set of teeth. Lost 'em at the Rev. Youngun's house at Thanksgivin', and he's been lookin' for 'em ever since."

Cubby came into the room. "Pops, I . . . Oh, hi, Miss Polly. I didn't know you were here."

"How you doin', Cubby?" she asked.

"Freezin' and fine," he laughed. "Never got this cold in St. Louis."

"You just stay inside, and it'll be over before you know it."

"You ready?" Dr. George asked. "Cubby, you better be makin' that list for Santa."

Polly laughed. "Get your letter off quick, or he won't know what you want."

Cubby shook his head. "Ain't no such thing as Santa. He's just make-believe."

On the outside steps, Polly began to pull her muffler over her face. "Shame he don't believe in Santa."

"He lost a lot of dreams when his momma died."

"But Christmas is a magic time," she said, covering her face. "You talk to that boy and show him the magic of love—Pops." She pulled the muffler up to her eyes before he could see her expression.

As they struggled through the snow to the hotel, Dr. George

noticed the strength of Polly's step. She was a strong woman, just like his mother.

Four-Eyes Johnson was sitting with his ankle propped up behind the check-out desk of the hotel. He looked up at the sound of footsteps. "Blondie, ith that you?" he shouted out.

Dr. George looked at Polly and whispered, "Blondie?"

Polly chuckled quietly. "Fool man thinks I'm from Sweden or somethin'. Been callin' me Blondie since the first day he met me."

"We need more half-blind good white men like him," he winked.

"Blondie, ith that you?" Four-Eyes shouted again.

"Yes, sir. I got you the doctor, like you asked." She leaned over and whispered into Dr. George's ear, "Without his teeth, he can't pronounce his c's and s's."

Dr. George noticed a hint of perfume and found it pleasant. "So, you fell down the stairs," he said to Four-Eyes.

Four-Eyes shook his head. "No, I fell *up* the thtairth. Just than't figure out how I ended up down in the bathement. Muth have rolled from the front thtepth to the bath thtepth and then down."

"I see," said Dr. George, rolling his eyes. "Let's take a look at this ankle of yours."

Four-Eyes asked, "Thay, have you theen my falth teeth?"

"No, I haven't."

"Well, pleathe keep a tharp eye out for them." Four-Eyes winced in pain and shouted, "Outhh!" Dr. George had touched his sore ankle. "Pleathe be thareful!"

After a quick examination, Dr. George said, "You've got a bad sprain. You need to keep the ankle wrapped tight and stay off it as much as you can for the next two weeks." Reaching into his bag, he brought out a small bottle of pills. "Take two of these now and two before you go to sleep. This will help the pain so you can relax."

Four-Eyes took the pills. "How muthh I owe you, Dothtor? Blondie thaid you were the betht dothtor in all of Miththouri."

Dr. George looked at Polly, who turned her face away with a blush. "Well, Mr. Johnson, how about a meal for two in your hotel dining room?"

"If you order the thpethial, then it'th a deal. You pay the ethtra if you want the thteak," Four-Eyes said.

"We'll go with the special," he laughed. "Polly, would you join me?" She nodded yes and beamed.

"You takin' Blondie to lunthh?" Four-Eyes asked with astonishment.

"I sure am. Or were you plannin' to ask her?"

"No. Withh I thould, but I'm too old. You treat my Blondie nithe, you hear?" As they walked toward the dining room, he shouted after them, "Keep thearthing for my teeth, pleathe."

They talked quietly over the lunch special of red beans, rice, and sliced sausage. Polly asked question after question, getting him to talk about his life, loves, and hurts.

"I've never told anyone what I've been tellin' you," he said with amazement.

"I'm a good listener, and you needed to talk to someone. I could see it in your eyes back at your house."

"Oh, that," he said, taking the last bite. "It's just Cubby."

"Is somethin' wrong?"

"No, it's just . . ." He stopped and looked out the window.

She finished the sentence for him. "It's just hard to bring a small boy into your private life."

Suddenly it all came out like a gushing river—his inability to really hug the boy and tell him that he loved him, that he felt bottled up, almost intimidated by intimacy.

Polly put her hand over his. "Men are raised to stumble."

"I don't understand."

"Men aren't taught to share their thoughts or show feelings. Men are supposed to be strong, not caring."

"My parents loved me."

"I'm sure they did, but do you ever hear anyone tell their child, 'Go cry on Daddy'? It's always the momma who hugs you and makes things better."

Dr. George thought back on his own upbringing and how his mother was the one who taught him about emotions. "My mother tried to teach me, but maybe I wasn't listenin'."

Polly squeezed his hand. "But you did listen! That's why things with Cubby are bothering you."

"You think so?" he asked hopefully.

"Sure. Sure I do," she said soothingly. "It's not wrong for a man to use words like *happy* or *sad*. It's not being weak to cry every now and then."

Dr. George felt the squeeze of her hands. Hers was an honest emotion, and he didn't know what he was feeling. "Cubby's here, and I want to care for him. I don't want to treat him like a long-term visitor. But it's hard."

"Some things never get easier until you start. You're doin' the right thing in wonderin' and worryin'. Things will work out for you and Cubby 'cause you want them to work out."

Dr. George looked down. "He misses his momma. Talks 'bout her every day."

"That's good," she smiled, taking her hand back. "He needs to talk about it. It's his way of workin' things out in his mind."

"Mothers teach their children everythin'."

"Not everythin'," she said, shaking her head. "A momma can teach a boy to be a human being, but she can't teach him to be a man—a real man. Cubby had his momma to help him this far, and now he's got you to teach him to be a good man."

Dr. George tried to lighten the mood. "But movin' him in has put a crimp in my social life!"

"I bet it has," she smiled. "There's some good in everythin'."

CHAPTER 21

GATHER ALL TOGETHER

With the shortage of wood, the four churches in town agreed to combine services and rotate Sundays. Laura had remembered the practice, common on the prairies of her youth, and encouraged the congregations to join in a common effort to conserve.

In her December 15 column, she wrote a convincing piece that was accepted without much grumbling:

TIME TO GATHER ALL TOGETHER

With the shortage of wood and fuel, I think we should combine our Sunday services. I have spoken with Rev. Youngun, Father Walsh, Rev. Moses, and Rev. Jones about this, and they agreed.

If we gather all together, we not only conserve wood, but enjoy a way for all of us to reflect on how little the differences between us are.

In the days of my youth on the prairie, we made do with what we had. When there was no church building available in the territories, service was held in private homes, stores, billiard parlors, and—yes, I know this is shocking—even in saloons! The hat was passed no matter where they took place.

Within our lifetime, it was common practice for new settlements to cooperate and build a religious "Pantheon" in the middle of town. All the denominations were allowed to use it. Worship was a big occasion in the isolated towns. I attended many Catholic, Episcopal, and Congregational services because that was the service being held that week.

Just as there is not enough firewood to go around, there were not enough ministers to reach all the small frontier settlements. The coming of an itinerant preacher was usually an event as important as the arrival of a wagon train or dance show.

I still have a broadside in my memory trunk which reads (and the spelling errors are in the original):

■ ■ ■ ■ ■ ■ ■ ■
The Bishop Is Coming!

Let us all turn out to hear the Cathlic Bishop. He promeses to preachin English in a non-inflamitory way.

Donations to stay in town, not go to Rome. Silent wurship acceptable.

Services in Plum Grove Pantheon on Sunday at 11 a.m. and 8 P.M.

PLEASE LEAVE YOUR GUNS WITH THE USHER

Next service whenever the Methodist missionary wagon prayer train returns.
■ ■ ■ ■ ■ ■ ■ ■
Worship was attended by all the immigrants, regardless of their creed. With the relentless winter that has set upon us, gathering together makes sense. It is time we all prayed for relief from the cold.

The first Sunday community religious gathering was an experience in itself. Someone certainly had a sense of humor when he brought those who braved the biting cold together in Rev. Youngun's church.

While the winds whistled and howled outside, those who could make the mixed service and were not members of Rev. Youngun's church entered warily. For the Catholics it was a time to see what they'd only heard about, and for many of the Methodists, it was a time to sit next to real Catholics.

For the members of the African Methodist Episcopal Church, it was a time to sit with whites. There was so much peering back and forth at one another that it took a while to bring everyone to order.

Manly, Laura, and Rose barely made it before the doors closed and the service began. They squeezed into the back pew and held their coats on their laps, because space was limited and the coatrack was full.

Four-Eyes Johnson tapped Laura on the shoulder. "Glad to thee you."

"Good to see you, Mr. Johnson." Laura had heard about his missing teeth and asked, "Find your teeth yet?"

"No, I'm thtill lookin'," he whispered, shaking his head and opening his mouth to show her his gums.

Laura closed her eyes as if in prayer, shutting off the sight. She opened the hymnal and busied herself, hoping that Four-Eyes wouldn't ask her anything more.

The service was jointly presided over by the four town ministers, who were as different as night and day. Rev. Youngun sat in his woolen suit next to Father Walsh in his robes, who sat next to Rev. Moses in his somber Congregational Sunday suit. On the end was the Travelin' Rev. Jones, of the African Methodist Episcopal Church, resplendent in his red robes and slicked-back hair.

They nodded politely to one another and joined in with the prayers and singing. All of the religious men were used to being center stage in their own domains, so sharing the power took a bit of getting used to.

When Father Walsh flicked holy water onto the Irish who had taken the five front left pews, some of it hit the Congregationalists behind them. Seeing them cringe and duck, Father Walsh said loudly, "Why are ye afraid of holy water? Haven't you been baptized by Rev. Moses yet?"

Rev. Moses chuckled good-naturedly and whispered to Rev. Youngun, "If he starts lightin' candles, I'm leavin'."

Travelin' Rev. Jones overheard him and said, "Ask him to light the candles under your glued-to-the-floor white choir. Way they sing in slow motion's puttin' me to sleep."

"Is there a special hymn you'd like us to sing?" asked Rev. Youngun.

Travelin' Rev. Jones scratched his head, then smiled. "Think you folks can sing a little bit of 'Swing Low, Sweet Chariot'?"

"I'll have the choir sing it next," Rev. Youngun whispered back. He got up and went over to the choir director.

Manly leaned over to Rose and whispered, "This ain't goin' to work out. You watch."

"Why?" Rose whispered back.

"This is like mixin' oil and water."

The Methodists liked to sing their hymns in a quiet, reverent manner. No matter what song they were singing, the congregation stood very still, and the choir didn't sway an inch either way.

The choir began singing in their normal manner. "Swing low, sweet char-i-ot, Coming for to car-ry me home. . . ."

Out in the congregation, Eulla Mae whispered to Maurice, "They need some black people up there."

Maurice raised his eyes in mock indignation. "Black people up there? I bet this is the first time they ever had blacks in here!"

After several minutes, the Travelin' Rev. Jones stood up and tried to pump up the beat with his arms. The choir tried to go faster but were unsure of themselves. In exasperation, Travelin'

Rev. Jones threw up his arms. "Hold it! Hold it!" The choir came to a halt, and the eyes of the room were upon him.

He looked out, seeing the black faces assembled in the right middle pews. "We need to warm up this room." He began pointing to individuals to come forward. "You girls—Adella, Angel Dove, Ceatrice, Clevanna, Dina Dell, and Zeolla—you come forward here now."

As the women stood and struggled out of the pews, the Travelin' Rev. Jones began pointing out others. "You men, we need some bass up here. Apple Jerry, Busybee, Bizelle, Elijah, Mo Fatten, and Verpo, get your b. . . ." He caught himself, but a ripple of laughter swept through the room. "Ah, get your bodacious voices up here!"

The other three ministers were as shocked as their congregations, but no one said anything. They were amazed at the smiles and jostling going on as Travelin' Rev. Jones moved black people around until the assembled choir looked like a double-six domino.

Travelin' Rev. Jones tapped Father Walsh to stand beside him on one side and Rev. Moses on the other. "You boys clap to the beat—if you can," he laughed.

Then, with his arms above his head, he bowed his head for a moment of silent prayer, raised his head, and shouted, "Let's have church, y'all!"

The entire room filled with electricity. Travelin' Rev. Jones turned to the choir and said, "Adella, Verpo, *get that chariot movin'!*"

With claps and shouts the choir hit a fast-paced version of the hymn, and within moments the white choir members were swaying to the beat. Some of the whites had trouble keeping their hips moving in the right direction, but Apple Jerry and Dina Dell bumped everyone back into line. As the mood heated the room, the whole congregation began swaying and clapping to the music.

The kids in the church loved all the singing and clapping. It was fun when moving and squirming was part of the service!

The Younguns were sitting off by themselves, out of sight of their father. Terry had a dime novel called *Col. Rubio—Swordsman of the North* hidden behind his hymnbook and was just finishing up the story when a paper airplane landed on his lap.

He looked up to see two brown eyes looking at him from the pew ahead. On one side of the boy was Dr. George, and on the other was Eulla Mae's sister Polly.

"It's mine. Give it to me," the black boy said.

"Mine now," snickered Terry. "Finders keepers, losers weepers."

Larry elbowed his brother. "Hush. Pa will be mad if he sees you talkin' in church."

Terry looked around. Seemed now that everyone was talking or doing something. Some of the Congregationalists were praying out loud, and several of the African Methodist Episcopals were standing up with their arms raised to heaven, saying "Amen" to everything that the Travelin' Rev. Jones said.

Terry smiled to himself. He liked this kind of church. Elbowing his brother back, he said, "This place sounds like a schoolyard. This is great!"

"I want my plane back," said the black boy.

"What's your name?" Terry asked.

Dr. George looked over and whispered, "Cubby, turn 'round! You don't be doin' that in church."

When everyone stood for the next hymn, Cubby looked back, and Terry stuck his tongue out. "Watch this," he whispered to Cubby. He tossed the plane up into the air with a backhand motion. It caught on an updraft when someone opened the back door and sailed back toward them. Terry and Cubby watched the plane, wondering where it would come down.

Sheriff Peterson, the tallest man in the room, reared his head back to sneeze just as the plane was passing over him. The strength of the sneeze sent the plane into a series of loop-deloops before gliding across the podium just as Rev. Youngun raised up his arms and said, "It's time to let your love take flight."

Laughter rippled through the room. At the end of the service, the four ministers stood to say parting words to their congregations.

Rev. Moses asked for each to help their neighbors and take in the helpless. Rev. Youngun encouraged sharing, and Father Walsh called on the Knights of Columbus to begin watching out for the elderly.

Travelin' Rev. Jones was the last. He simply said, "It's a shame that we have to wait for a blizzard before we sit together as brothers."

As the service ended, the people bundled up against the cold and headed quickly home through the howling winds. Dr. George stopped Laura at the door. "I was up with Martha Helling yesterday. I think she's goin' to be deliverin' within the week."

"Has Jacob changed?" Laura asked.

"Man won't change, but the baby did. I'm sure it's goin' to be a breech birth." He shook his head. "That woman needs either a white doctor or a midwife. And since I'm the only doctor in this town and there ain't no midwife, looks like I'm electin' you."

"I told you, Doc, I don't know if I can do it."

"You *got* to do it."

Manly, who had listened to the conversation and knew of the mean streak inside Jacob Helling, quietly asked, "You want me to help, Doc? I've birthed calves and foals. Can't be that much different."

"Oh hush, Manly," Laura said. "Even I've done that!"

Dr. George pulled on his coat. "You have? Well, then, you can help birth a baby."

"Women aren't animals," Laura huffed.

"I know that," said Dr. George. "But you and I both know

they have babies pretty much the same way. Besides, you've given birth yourself, Laura. You know how it is firsthand."

Laura stamped her foot. "Doc, there's a big difference between having a baby and helping someone else have one. What if I don't want to do this? Can't you get someone else?" She looked at Polly, who had come up and was standing next to Dr. George. "Can't you take Polly with you?"

Manly took Laura's hand. "Laura, Jacob Helling's a mean black hater. Don't matter if it's a man or woman to him. He only sees the color."

Dr. George nodded. "Manly's right, Laura. Helling's a racist. Black, brown, or yellow, he hates us all. Can't reason with people like that."

Manly held up Laura's coat. "Doc, if she don't do it, I will."

"I'll do it! I've had enough of you two! Just leave me alone!" she snapped, walking out of the church by herself.

"What'th wrong with her?" Four-Eyes asked as she brushed by him. "Thay, hath anyone theen my teeth?"

CHAPTER 22

THREE DAYS BEFORE CHRISTMAS

As the snow continued to pile up, Mansfield lost a lot of its Christmas spirit. Mail wasn't getting in or out, and the Sears shipment of toys to Bedal's General Store hadn't arrived. With the rail lines closed, people were more concerned with staying warm and keeping fed than with preparing for Christmas.

Three days before Christmas, shrieking winds tore through the town, rattling the windows and blowing over the weather vanes that had not already broken off from the ice. This was a sign of a bad storm, so farmers began waking up their animals and keeping them moving, so they wouldn't freeze.

A family of three froze to death in the storm during the night, when their shanty caught fire and they tried to get to their neighbor's house. The numbing winds and driving snow disoriented them, and they were found beside a tree just fifty yards from their destination. The snow had been so thick that they hadn't been able to see the house.

Several farmers suffered frostbitten ears, fingers, and toes, so Dr. George was working overtime. His supply of painkillers was running low, and he'd begun cutting clean sheets into bandages, just in case someone needed an emergency operation.

Sheriff Peterson brought in a Polish immigrant whose left index finger had come off from frostbite. The man was half-crazy, screaming in Polish and English. After they'd been trapped in his wagon for three days without food, he had finally left his wife and child huddled in the wagon and tried to walk to town for help. The sheriff had found his wife and child dead.

The dead were taken to the Morgan Funeral Home. Curly Joe Thomas, the undertaker's assistant, carried them in saying, "Can't bury no one until the ground thaws."

A storage shed behind the funeral home had been converted into a morgue. Bodies were placed throughout the room in the frozen positions they'd been found. It was a terrifying sight that Curly Joe would remember for the rest of his life.

Manly and Laura were in Mansfield, having brought baskets of apples and potatoes from their root cellar to share with the needy. The new blizzard that swept through town was so strong that they had to take refuge in the hotel until it subsided.

"You thay'in the night?" Four-Eyes asked.

Laura shook her head. "No, Mr. Johnson. We're going to sit in your lobby until the storm lets up." Seeing him rub his gums, Laura asked, "Still haven't found your teeth yet, huh?"

"No-thir-re-bob, thtill haven't found 'em!"

When the winds died down and the snow let up, Manly and Laura got into their cutter and headed back toward home. They were making good speed across the new snow, when the blizzard began again as they reached Willow Creek Bridge.

The winds were so strong that the driving snow felt like needles. The horses reared up, so Manly struggled to the front of the sleigh and covered their eyes with his muffler and Laura's woolen scarf.

The temperature dropped rapidly, and it took them an hour to cover a ten-minute distance. Laura nodded off against

Manly's shoulder, her lap robe covered by a thick three-inch crust of snow and her lips blue.

"Wake up, Laura. Wake up!" Manly shouted over the wind. "Don't fall asleep on me now, girl!"

He kept shaking her, but the cold had grabbed her rapidly. In desperation, he took off his coat and wrapped it around her, then stood on the front of the sleigh, cracking his whip above the wind. "Faster! Move now! Don't let the ice grab, boys," he shouted to the horses.

When they reached Apple Hill, Manly pulled into the barn and carried Laura from the sleigh. Rose saw them coming and held open the door.

"Is Mother all right?" she said loudly.

"Get some coffee going and a pot of hot water," he shouted, carrying Laura into the parlor. He laid her out in front of the fireplace and shook off the snowy robe.

"Come on, Laura. It's over now. You're going to be all right."

He rubbed her hands and feet. Rose brought in the warm water, and they took wet rags and rubbed them on her body. She slowly came around. "Manly?"

"Take it easy, girl. You just took the cold too fast."

Laura looked disoriented, blinking her eyes and looking around. "I felt as if I were going to sleep. Such a peaceful sleep."

"You're all right now. You're all right now," he said, hugging her close.

Rose stood in the doorway, looking at her parents by the fire. There was so much love in the room that it overwhelmed her, and she began to cry.

Manly looked up at the sound and waved her over. Rose knelt down beside them, and Manly wrapped her in their embrace.

CHAPTER 23

IS SANTA COMIN'?

With just three days to go before Christmas, the children of Mansfield were worried that Santa might not make it to town.

When the storm stopped, the Younguns went to work on some Santa signs. Their hands nearly froze aligning rocks and poles into twenty-foot letters reading:

SANTA ━ ━ ━ ━ ＞
STOP HERE! ━ ━ ━ ━ ＞

They also shoveled off part of the barn roof to paint an arrow. Their idea seemed pretty good, but the can of red paint froze halfway through, and they had to give up.

Sherry left carrot and cookie trails for Santa's reindeer to find the house, a trail the snow rabbits ate. Terry schemed a way to get extra toys. He was hanging socks and underwear from the pine tree in the front yard when Larry came out.

"What are you doin'?" Larry asked.

Terry grinned. "Santa will see the undie tree and feel sorry for us. Think we're too poor for ornaments. I bet we'll get lots of extra toys."

With cookies left on plates and the landing spot on the roof they'd cleared for Santa's sleigh, the Younguns felt that Santa would surely be able to find them.

While the three Younguns were standing on the porch, admiring their Santa signs, the blizzard struck again, covering over everything they'd done.

"How's Santa ever goin' to find our house?" wailed Terry. "The whole world is covered with snow."

Larry nodded. "I thought he'd be able to see our sign, but the snow's covered it."

Sherry moaned, "What are we goin' to do?"

Terry scratched his head. "Think he just knows where we live?"

"Do you even know our address?" asked Larry.

"No, but . . ."

Then it hit Larry. "That's it! We forgot to write Santa a letter tellin' him what we want and where we live."

"What would we say?" Sherry asked.

Terry started talking as if he were an old hand at writing Santa. "You tell him all kinds of things 'bout how good you've been, how you don't fib, and . . ."

"You might as well send him a blank piece of paper," Larry said, shaking his head.

Sherry stuck her tongue out. "Fibbers don't get presents from Santa!"

Terry started to bop her, but Larry grabbed his arm. "You don't hit girls," he said harshly.

"That's what I'm goin' to put in my letter to Santa," Terry said, nodding up and down. "Uh-huh, that's what I want!"

"What?" asked Sherry innocently.

"I want one chance to really bop you a good one for everythin' you've done to me!" he exclaimed, jumping at her.

"Larry, keep him off me!" she screamed, clinging to her older brother's legs.

Larry grabbed Terry by the collar and lifted him off the ground. "Stop it! Stop it! Pa'll hear and we'll get nothin' but switches and coal for Christmas."

"Switches and coal?" asked Sherry. "Who'd want that?"

"Nobody would," Larry answered, "but that's what you get if you're bad. Santa knows. *He knows everything.*"

"Think he knows about the smoked turkey?" Terry asked, looking down.

"Yup, so you best be extra good, or you'll get nothin' this year."

The children began writing their letters to Santa. Larry wrote his. Terry attempted to write his, and Sherry drew a picture of what she wanted, with a note from Larry attached. Larry's letter was short, and to the point:

Deer Santa:
   I'm tired of tryinn to ride Crab Apple the mule. He bites my behind when I get on and off him. Would you pleaze bringe me a horse?
Your friend Larry Youngun
P.S. Please look carefulie for our houze as it is covered with snow.

Larry sealed his letter up and addressed the envelope to:

Santa Klause, North Poll.

Terry's letter was a bit more creative, because he was worried about what Santa may have seen during the year:

Deare Sanna:
Gues u no that I been studyinn to be an actor. Had 2 play lots of practise rolls as a bad boy dis yeer. Hope i didnnt fool u!

> *I lost mi pokut nife inn the woods trying to save Tede Rooozefelt. Bring mee another one, pleazzz.*
> *Ur good boy,*
> *Terry Youngun*

He sealed up his envelope and addressed it to:

SANNA, NOR POLL

Sherry handed her picture to Larry, who knew what it was supposed to be. "You want this?" he asked.

Sherry nodded, looking at the picture of a pink pig with a ribbon on. "I want another Bessie," she said with determination.

"But Bessie's dead," Larry said sadly.

"Santa will bring anything I want. And that's what I want!"

Larry reluctantly took the picture and wrote this note beside it:

> *Deer Santa:*
> *My sester Sherry wans a Bessie pig jus like this picture. Ok? Sherry loved Bessie but she waz killed for ham hocks by mees-take. She's in heaven if you kin find her. Thanks Santa.*
> *Sherry's brother Larry.*

Larry reopened his envelope and stuck Sherry's letter in. "Now, let's go mail them."

"Where?" Sherry asked.

"In town. Got to mail them in town," Larry said, picking up his coat. Terry grabbed his, not realizing Four-Eyes' teeth were in the thick hood of his winter coat.

They hitched their sled behind Crab Apple the mule, who looked kind of silly in the red and white stocking cap they'd stuck on his head. The two ear holes they'd cut out held his ears close to his head, but if a mule could look embarrassed, Crab Apple looked embarrassed.

"Crab Apple looks like a reindeer," Sherry said.

The mule snorted, and Terry laughed. "If that's what a reindeer looks like, I know Santa won't make it here!"

"Why?" asked Larry.

" 'Cause Santa would never make it out of the North Pole if he had a team of reindeer as ornery as Crab Apple!"

The wind was quite strong, but Crab Apple pulled them along through the snowdrifts. They'd left Dangit locked in the barn and could hear him howling over the wind.

About halfway to the Willow Creek Bridge, they heard barking and yipping behind them. Dangit was racing through the snow!

"That fool dog won't leave us alone," Terry said with icy breath.

Dangit made a flying leap and missed the sled, diving straight into a snowbank. He disappeared into the deep snow.

"Where's Dangit?" Sherry asked.

Larry got off the sled and began digging into the snow. About two feet in, he saw Dangit's stubby tail and pulled on it, lifting the dog out. Larry dusted the snow off him.

"If we hadn't seen you go into the snow, you'd be a dead duck," Larry scolded him.

"No, a dead Dangit," Sherry corrected.

The wind gusted up, and a tree dumped snow on their heads. Terry shook it off, complaining. "Come on, come on! Let's get to town and mail the letters."

He took the letter from his pocket and held it up. "Santa, please don't leave the North Pole until you get my letter," he wished aloud.

He put the letter away, and as they approached the Willow Creek Bridge, they saw some of the Hardacres boys pushing an enormous log over the side. It broke through the ice, jutting out at an angle, with a web of ice cracks extending in all directions.

The Hardacres boys laughed and slipped down the bank. They went up the solid part of the frozen creek, sliding and laughing on the ice.

As Crab Apple pulled their sled onto the Willow Creek Bridge, the wind whipped up and they were momentarily blinded by snow flurries. When it cleared, Terry took out his letter again. "Larry, don't we need to put a stamp on this?"

Larry turned and replied, "Naw, Santa pays all the postage."

Another gust of wind came down the center of the bridge and took the letter from Terry's hands. He cried out as the letter floated off the bridge and over onto the ice. It landed at the deepest point, right under the bridge, surrounded by the ice cracks. Terry jumped off the sled and ran off the bridge and down the bank.

"Stop, Terry! Don't go on the ice!" Larry shouted.

"I got to get my letter!" Terry screamed back. "If Santa don't get it, he won't know what I want!"

Terry started out onto the ice, slipping and sliding until he got to his letter. He picked it up, clutching it in his hand as if it were a million dollars.

Larry looked over the rail and saw the cracks. "Stop right there. Don't move!" he yelled.

"Why?" Terry shouted back. Suddenly he noticed the ice cracks.

"The ice is cracked!" Larry shouted. "Lay down and back up slowly."

Terry froze in place. "I can't move," he whimpered. "I'm scared."

The ice cracked around him like a gunshot. A big piece broke away, leaving Terry under the bridge on a four-foot-wide ice peninsula.

"Do something!" Sherry cried out.

"I'm tryin'," Larry said. He looked back down at Terry.

"Don't move. I'm goin' to take the reins off Crab Apple and pull you back up."

The ice cracked again as the log slipped into the water. "Hurry, I'm about to wet my pants!" Terry cried.

Larry frantically began to unhook the sled reins from Crab Apple. He didn't hear the sleigh bells coming down Hardacres road, which was the old way to get to Springfield. Kris Kringle, the jolly mailman, had finished his last mail run before the holidays.

Kris sized up the situation immediately when he saw Larry swinging the reins down toward the little boy on the thin finger of ice. If the boy fell through the ice, he'd die for sure. Kris stood up in the sleigh and cracked the whip. "Let's go, girls. Move it!" he shouted to his team of horses.

Larry swung the reins, but Terry missed them. "Don't move. I'll get them into your hands. Hold tight when I do, and Crab Apple and I'll pull you up."

"Hurry," Terry whimpered, as the ice cracked again. He turned at the sound of sleigh bells and stood there with his mouth open.

Sherry heard the sleigh bells and stared in shock. Larry didn't turn to look, but asked over his shoulder, "Who's comin'?"

"Santa," she whispered. "Santa Claus is comin' to the rescue!"

Coming down the hill on a fast sleigh flying over the snow, Kris Kringle certainly must have looked like Santa. He was standing up, with his red stocking cap on, cracking his whip, with his long white hair and beard.

"Well, I'll be," Larry muttered. "Santa Claus."

The ice cracked again. Terry screamed, "Quit thinkin' 'bout presents and tell Santa to fly down here and save me!"

Kris Kringle pulled his sleigh to a sliding halt in the middle of the bridge. "We got to move fast, all right?" Neither Larry nor Sherry could say a thing. "Do you children speak English?" he asked them.

From below the bridge came Terry's voice, "I'll speak any durn language you want, Santa! Fly down here and save me. Help!"

Kris Kringle took a coiled rope from under his bench seat and went to the side of the bridge. He made a loop and tossed it to Terry, saying, "Grab this, slip it over your head, and put your arms through it. Understand?"

Terry nodded as the ice cracked again. "Hurry, Santa! Hurry!"

Kris Kringle missed with his first toss, and Terry almost fell off the ice patch trying to grab it.

"Don't move! I'll get this to you," Kris said. He motioned to Larry. "Grab the end of the rope behind me and pull when I tell you to."

"What about me, Santa?" Sherry asked.

Kris's pudgy cheeks crinkled with his smile. "Just sing a song or something. Everything's goin' to be all right."

"Is 'Joy to the World' all right, Santa?"

Kris Kringle coiled the rope for another toss. "Fine, girl. I like that song."

Sherry belted out the first verse of the song as the rope sailed through the air. Terry watched it float toward him. He was praying that it would get to him before the spreading ice cracked under his feet.

He reached up on his tiptoes and grabbed the rope, bringing it over his head and under his arms, all in one motion. At the exact moment that Kris and Larry pulled Terry into the air, the ice patch broke into a mass of fragments.

Sherry was singing her heart out as Terry was pulled over the edge of the bridge. Kris Kringle lifted him up over the rail and plopped him down on the icy bridge. "Now, would someone mind tellin' me what you were doin' out on the cracked ice?"

Terry looked down, saw the letter to Santa clutched in his hand, and raised it up with a smile. "I had to get your letter."

"My letter?" asked Kris in astonishment.

"Yeah. We were writin' you, tellin' you what we wanted for Christmas," said Larry.

Kris took the letter from Terry and saw that it was addressed to Santa. Larry handed him his and Sherry's.

Larry looked at Kris with wonder in his eyes. "We were just goin' into town to mail these to you."

"Yeah," Sherry exclaimed, "we were worried that they wouldn't get to you in time."

"Yeah, too much snow," said Terry. "We thought you wouldn't be able to find our house."

"Well, children," Kris said, "Santa needs his letters, and I always find the right homes."

"Can you bring what we want?" asked Sherry.

"Why, young lady, I haven't read your letter yet. Have you been a good girl?"

"I'm always good. It's Terry who's bad," she said, pointing to her brother.

"Is that so?" Kris asked, looking at Terry seriously.

Terry squirmed around nervously, pulling at his ears and blinking his eyes. "I've been tryin' to be good, but sometimes it's hard. Little boys with red hair seem born for trouble sometimes."

Kris nodded. "I'll take your hair into account when I add up everything you've done this year."

"Can I sit on your sleigh, Santa?" Terry asked.

"Just for a moment, son."

Terry climbed up and pretended to be guiding the sleigh through the sky. He leaned backward and fell over the seat, and Four-Eyes' teeth slipped from his hood, lodging between two mail sacks.

Kris Kringle turned to Larry. "How about you, son? Have you been good?"

Larry shuffled his cold feet. "I've tried, Santa. But if you can't bring me what I want . . ." he paused and put his arm around Sherry, "please bring Sherry what she wants. She's been hurt bad and really needs it."

"And where can I get what you want?" Kris asked.

Sherry looked up toward the sky with an icy tear on her face. "Heaven."

Kris took a deep breath and looked down at the three faces. "Okay, children. I'll take your letters back to the North Pole and read them. If you are good between now and Christmas morning, I think Santa will make you happy."

Kris got back up on his sleigh. "Now, stay off the ice! Go home and get warm, you understand?"

"Yes, Santa," Larry and Terry answered in unison.

Sherry didn't say a word. She just stood there, shaking her head. Kris laughed, "And what are you shaking your head about, young lady?"

"Somethin's not right," she said bluntly.

"And what's that?" Kris asked.

Larry tried to silence her, but she pushed his arm away. "I've never heard of Santa havin' his sleigh pulled by horses. Where are your reindeer?"

Kris laughed. "When I'm out West here, I sometimes use horses. My reindeer are back at the North Pole, resting up for the big run." He sat on the sleigh bench and cracked his whip. "Okay, Max and Tulip, let's go!"

The mail sleigh pulled off with a flurry of snow. "Max and Tulip?" Larry asked out loud.

Terry stamped his feet to get warm. "I don't care if he calls his horses and reindeer Dangit and Crab Apple. Santa just gave me a good-behavior pass for the year. I know I'll get my knife now! I just know it!"

CHAPTER 24

ALL I WANT FOR CHRISTMAS

K̲ris Kringle parked his sleigh behind the Mansfield Hotel, unhitched his team of horses, and had the livery boy take them in and feed them.

There were only two mail sacks left, and the day was about over, so he reached in to pick them up and take them to his room for the night. He heard something hit the bottom of the sleigh as he lifted the sacks over the sleigh rail.

Looking down, he saw a set of false teeth. "Must have fallen out of one of the packages," he said to himself. He put the false teeth into his jacket pocket and walked to the hotel's front door.

The welcome warmth of the hotel lobby made him blink, but he kept his hat and coat on, because he was still cold. There was no one at the desk, so he tapped the desk bell for service.

"Anybody here?" Kris asked loudly.

"Keep your thhirt on. Hold your hortheth," came a voice from the office behind the partition.

Four-Eyes had been holed up in his small office, wishing he

had his teeth. There wasn't anything on earth that he wanted more at that moment.

Since he lost his teeth on Thanksgiving, he hadn't been able to eat solid foods. He was plumb tired of eating soup, oatmeal, and mushy toast, so he had been sitting in his tiny office, wishing that Santa Claus or someone would hear his prayers and bring him some new teeth. He walked out and stopped.

Kris smiled warmly. "Any room at the inn for a cold, hungry stranger?"

Four-Eyes peered through his thick glasses. His whole world was always blurry, but he focused on the red hat, long white hair, and full beard. Then he saw that the man was big and chubby and had rosy cheeks.

"What are you staring at?" laughed Kris.

"You look jutht like . . ." Four-Eyes stuttered.

"You're right. My name's Kris Kringle."

Four-Eyes went weak at the knees. *Kris Kringle,* he thought to himself! That was the name he'd used for Santa Claus at his grandmother's home. She was from Norway and told him all the Kris Kringle tales about how Santa sometimes wore disguises to sneak into towns and check on people.

"Thanta!" he cried out, "Thanta! You heard my Thhrithtmath prayerth!"

Four-Eyes hobbled out from around the desk and hugged Kris Kringle. "Did you bring my prethent, Thanta?"

Kris felt awkward with the old man hugging him, but he knew that the loneliness of holidays had strange effects on people. He felt sorry for the toothless old man with the thick glasses. "I can't give you your present now. It's not Christmas yet."

Four-Eyes stepped back, looking Kris up and down. "Oh Thanta, than't you make an extheption thith time? I lotht my teeth and need 'em bad."

"I see," said Kris. Then he brightened, thinking about the

false teeth he'd found in the sleigh. "You need some new teeth, huh?"

Four-Eyes beamed. "I thure do, and you know it, because I've been thayin' my Thanta prayerth every night thinthe Dethember firtht, thutht like Grandma taught me."

"Well, my good man," Kris said, puffing up his chest, "Christmas is only a few days away. If I made an exception for you, why . . ." he paused and spread his arms out, "I'd have to make exceptions for millions of children around the world. You can wait two more days, can't you?"

Four-Eyes shuffled his feet. "I guethth tho. Jutht that I'm hungry and can't even eat my own two-pound T-bone theak thpethial in the rethtaurant."

Kris' eyes widened. "Did you say two-pound T-bone steak?"

Four-Eyes had a look of joy on his face. "Gothh, you mutht be hungry, Thanta. Tired of all thothe milk and thootieth, huh?"

Kris nodded. "Too many cookies gives me gas. But that steak sounds great. Let me check in first, and then I'll take one rare with all the trimmin's."

He signed the register with a flourish, but Four-Eyes wouldn't take any money. "The roomth free and tho ith the meal, Thanta. All I want for Thhrithtmath is my new teeth."

Kris put his hand into his pocket and felt the teeth. *What if they don't fit?* he thought to himself. Well, he'd wait for the answer until Christmas morning. The man had asked for teeth, which is what Kris would give him.

As he sat down to eat, he took out his pocketknife and opened the Younguns' letters. He read Terry's first. *This boy has trouble with the truth,* he thought to himself, rereading part of the letter. "I lost my pocketknife in the woods, trying to save Teddy Roosevelt." *This boy should be a lawyer when he grows up,* Kris thought.

Kris looked at the pocketknife in his hand. "Well," he said

out loud, "guess this is a message to share. I'll just give him my own knife."

Heck, he'd saved the boy's life so maybe there was a reason for everything that had been happening lately. Kris had never been much of a church-going man, but he decided that some prayers might be in order if the Man upstairs was sending him a signal.

He then picked up Larry's letter. *Horse?* he thought. *That's a tall order for a young boy. Where am I going to get a horse with three days left before Christmas? This request might not be filled,* he thought, shaking his head.

Then he pulled out Sherry's picture of the pink pig and smiled. Gosh, how he loved ham—ham cooked any way: baked, smoked, cured, fried, boiled, stewed, it didn't matter.

Eating ham was like chewing on a little piece of heaven. All he could think about was a hot ham sandwich, until he read what Sherry wanted. *A pig? Why couldn't she have asked for something simple like a doll?* he thought. The waiter brought him his T-bone steak, and Kris put the letter away. He'd think about it later.

After the wonderful meal, Kris walked through the lobby and started up the stairs. Four-Eyes came out from his office and called out, "Pleathe don't forget about my new falthe teeth."

"Thure won't," Kris said without thinking.

CHAPTER 25

TWO DAYS BEFORE CHRISTMAS

Dr. George had picked up Rev. Youngun to go with him to visit the Hellings. The baby was overdue, and Martha Helling was nearly delirious.

Cubby and the Youngun children were left at the Mansfield Hotel, along with Crab Apple, who was put into the hotel's stable. The kids had wanted to keep Dangit the dog in their room, but it was against hotel policy, so Dangit was kept in a cage in the barn, next to their mule.

"He ain't gonna like that," Terry said, shaking his head.

Rev. Youngun said, "He's got no choice. It's either that or freeze outside on the porch."

Polly had said she'd watch the Youngun children for the day, and Mr. Johnson had offered to pay them to look for his teeth.

"I'll give thomeone a dollar if they find my teeth fatht," he said, spraying spittle on Larry's face.

While Rev. Youngun told his three children to be good, Cubby hugged Dr. George. "When you goin' to be back, Pops?"

"We'll be back by nightfall. Now you be good, all right?" Dr. George said.

Polly laughed. "I'll watch 'em all. Don't you worry."

Cubby eyed the three Youngun children and recognized Terry. "Pops, that's the redhead who wouldn't give my paper airplane back in church!"

"Finders keepers," Terry snickered, sticking his tongue out between his hands so his pa wouldn't see it.

"You best find this," Cubby said, cocking his fist. Terry jumped up and down, tossing air punches.

"Stop it!" Dr. George boomed out. "There'll be no fightin'. You're neighbors, so get along!"

Cubby hugged Dr. George's leg. "Three against one ain't fair, Pops." He turned and gave a mean eye to Terry.

Rev. Youngun pushed his children forward. "No need for it to be that way. How 'bout four together instead?"

"How 'bout forget it?" Terry mumbled, tossing one more air punch.

Dr. George shook his head at Polly. "Think you can handle 'em?"

Four-Eyes laughed. "Blondie? The day she than't handle four little white boyth will be the day I than't thee my nothe."

Sherry tugged at his sleeve. "Mr. Johnson, I'm Sherry, and I'm a girl."

Four-Eyes looked down and patted the top of her head, "Oh, I thought you were that third brother of yourth I met at Thankthgiving."

"Third brother?" Dr. George asked Rev. Youngun quietly.

"I'll explain it later," Rev. Youngun whispered back.

Dr. George reached out and took Polly's hands in his and held them. "Thanks. We'll be back before dark. Would you like to have dinner with me?"

Polly's eyes danced. "That would be nice." Cubby saw the look that passed between them and nuzzled against Polly.

It was a cold sleigh ride as they left the outskirts of Mansfield. Shrieking winds whipped them back and forth, and thick clouds blocked the sun.

"Maybe you can talk some sense into her husband," Dr. George said. "She needs a doctor and, black or not, I'm the only one around."

"You think I'll be able to talk sense into him? That man is so filled with hatred it scares me."

They rode on silently until they got to Willow Creek Bridge. Rev. Youngun looked over. "Are you sure you should be takin' Laura with us? She doesn't want to do it, from what I've heard."

"She's strong, got respect 'round here, and is not afraid to argue with a man when she knows she's right. I think things are going to get rough up there if that baby won't come out normal. Might have to do a cesarean."

"Cesarean," Rev. Youngun said, whistling. "That should be done in a hospital."

Dr. George nodded. He didn't know how on earth he could surgically open the mother and remove her baby without touching Martha Helling himself. "It should be done in a hospital, yes," he said. "But there ain't no hospital around. And there weren't any around when Julius Caesar was born the very same way centuries ago, but he made it, alive and kickin'."

"Can't you move the baby around or somethin'?" Rev. Youngun asked, making a face.

"If the baby won't come out normally, then we got no choice."

Rev. Youngun shook his head. "You think Laura can perform the operation?"

"That's why you're along," Dr. George said.

"Me? I can't do it!"

Dr. George looked into his eyes. "No, but you're strong enough to hold Jacob Helling down when the time comes. I'll perform the operation, all right. I just can't fight him off and deliver the baby at the same time."

"Have you told Laura this?" Rev. Youngun asked.

"Naw," he said, shaking his head. "She's just my insurance, in case it takes the both of us to hold off Jacob."

Laura was bundled and ready when they arrived at Apple Hill Farm. Manly waved good-bye as the three of them whisked through the frigid air toward the Hellings'.

Laura grumped, "I couldn't sleep a wink last night, thinking about delivering this baby."

Dr. George laughed. "You'll do just fine. The first thing you do is . . ."

Laura interrupted him. "The first thing I'm going to do is talk some sense into that stubborn cuss! No man has the right to endanger his wife that way. Women aren't property, you know!"

Rev. Youngun leaned over and whispered to Dr. George, "Won't need firewood to keep the cabin warm. I think we're in for some red-hot fireworks."

"I heard that!" Laura said, crossing her arms.

As they sleighed in silence through the hollow and worked their way around the snowdrifts, life was going from bad to worse for Jacob and Martha Helling. Food and fuel were running low, along with patience and hope.

They'd burned most of the firewood and were resorting to "prairie logs," which were leg-sized bundles of hay wrapped in string. They burned bright, hot, and fast, but were very dangerous. It was either that or begin burning the furniture, which Jacob wasn't about to do.

Between Martha's pains and the sow and her piglets near freezing to death, Jacob Helling had not gotten much sleep. If he didn't keep the animals awake at night, they might freeze, and if he didn't keep his wife warm, she'd die.

Martha had cried out so many times that he'd almost become used to it. This scream was different. He could hear it from the barn. He poured a bucket of feed for the sow and dashed back toward the house. She screamed again, and it seemed to shake the snow off the trees.

"Martha. Martha, are you all right?" he cried out, rushing to her bedside.

Her face was ashen, with a thin film of perspiration across her lip. "It hurts bad, Jacob. Feels like the baby wants to come out but can't," she moaned.

He felt her extended stomach and saw the baby kick. "He's movin' 'round a lot. Maybe he's not ready to come out just yet and is lettin' you know it."

"He?" She smiled weakly. "What makes you think it's a he?"

"Just got a feelin' in the bones, that's all," he said.

"When's the doctor goin' to get here? Have you heard?"

"Said he'd be here this morning. And I'll say one thing for that black man, he's always here when he says he'll be."

"He's a doctor! Just 'cause he's black don't mean nothin'," she said, gritting her teeth.

Jacob shook his head. "Color means everything to me. That's just how it is."

He walked over to the fireplace and shoved another large prairie log into the fire. The hay ignited quickly, lighting up the room. A small piece of burning hay floated on the heat waves near the screen. Jacob clapped it between his hands, putting it out.

"Be careful with those prairie logs," Martha said weakly.

CHAPTER 26

LIFE OR DEATH

Sheriff Peterson reached for another bag of food from the back of his cutter. He was bone tired but some of these families would starve without his deliveries. Pride and determination kept him going.

The poor Okie family eagerly took the food, then locked the door behind them, trying to protect what little warmth they had left in their cabin. The sheriff clapped his hands together to keep the circulation going as he climbed back into his sleigh to make the last delivery.

The winds of another blizzard were picking up, making for very slow travel with limited visibility. If he hadn't been looking around at that exact moment, the sheriff wouldn't have seen the snow-buried figure on the side of the road.

He pulled the sleigh to a sliding halt and jumped off. He recognized the man as Boris Kamarov, a Russian Jew who had settled in a remote corner of the valley with his wife and two children.

"Kamarov! Kamarov, wake up!" Peterson shouted, shaking the snow off the half-frozen man. It appeared that the man was trying to speak, so Peterson put his ear near his lips. The howling wind was too loud, so the sheriff picked the man up and carried him back to his cutter.

Kamarov started to moan. "They freezing," he whispered. "Help them."

"What did you say?"

Kamarov tried to point up toward the road he'd come down in the blizzard before he passed out in the woods. From behind them the sheriff heard sleigh bells and saw Dr. George's large cutter coming up the pass.

He stopped next to the sheriff. "What's wrong, Sheriff?" Dr. George asked.

"Doc, take a look at this man. I think he's got frostbite."

Dr. George looked at the man's face and felt his fingers. "This man needs to be warmed up quick. Take him back to town, soak him in a warm bath, and give him some coffee."

Laura brought over one of her two lap robes and wrapped it around the Russian. "This man's going to die. You've got to get him back now."

The sheriff shook his head. "Can't. Before he passed out he said his wife and children were freezin'. They live right up over the ridge here."

Rev. Youngun came over. "Sheriff, I'll come with you to get his family. Doc, you and Laura go on to the Hellings'. I'll see you back in town tonight."

The road divided about forty yards ahead, and as they parted company, Laura waved half-heartedly. A feeling of dread came over her as the blizzard began again with deadly fury.

As they neared the Helling cabin, Dr. George looked at the stark building set against the deepening snow. Any other cabin with a fireplace going would have been a welcome sight, but there was no welcome for him in Helling's cabin.

Laura saw the look of consternation on his face and said, "It can't be any colder in there than it is out here. You talked me into this, so let's get it over."

Inside the cabin, Jacob Helling announced, "That doctor's back. Brought along that Wilder woman, who talks back to men and writes all that nonsense."

"Laura Wilder is out there?" Martha asked weakly, touching her hair.

Jacob made a face and mocked her tone. "Yeah, Laura Wilder's out there!"

Pain wracked her body, and she cried out against it.

Jacob rushed to her side. "Martha, what can I do?"

Martha gulped for air and moistened her lips. She whispered, "Get that doctor in here, Jacob. I need a man who'll help me, and I don't care if he's white or black," she whispered, with a look of fury in her eyes.

CHAPTER 27

HOTEL DISASTER

hile Cubby, Larry, and Sherry were playing hide-and-go-seek with Polly, Terry struck up a conversation with an old roustabout named Farley. The blizzard was blowing too hard for Farley to get over to Tippy's Saloon, so he was waiting for the storm to subside in the hotel lobby, having a chew, and playing cards.

"Whatcha playin'?" Terry asked, standing by the table.

Farley looked over at the auburn-haired boy. "Red, I'm playin' solitaire, if that's all right with you."

"Fine by me," Terry said. "Can I play?"

Farley spit into the spitoon. "Solitaire means by yourself. No little snots allowed into the game." He spit again. "Why don't you go pester your momma or somethin' and leave me alone?"

"Can't."

"Can't what?" He put the cards down and took out a pair of dice and rolled out snake eyes.

"Can't leave, 'cause my daddy told me not to. Can't pester my momma 'cause she's dead."

Terry's blunt answer caught Farley off guard. He'd been an

orphan himself. He pulled up a chair. "So you want to learn to play cards, do ya? Well, first thing a boy needs to know about is craps. You know how to play craps?" he asked, shaking the dice.

"Craps? Who wants to play that?" Terry asked making a face.

Farley rolled out a seven. "Hot darn, a seven! This is my lucky day!" He looked at Terry. "Kid, I'm talkin' 'bout dice, craps, the man's game of chance. Now sit down here and I'll teach you how to earn a good livin' without workin'."

Farley rolled again, this time an eleven. He looked over at Terry. "You got any money, Red?"

"Got my allowance," Terry said, jingling the coins in his pocket.

"Good, 'cause you might have to pay for me educatin' you," Farley said with a sneaky glint in his eye.

Meanwhile, Sherry had tired of the hide-and-seek game and noticed the bell on the hotel's counter. She pulled herself up and slapped the bell several times. "Checkin' in!" she shouted, just as she'd heard the last man say.

"Hold your horteth," Four-Eyes said from his office. "I'll be right there."

He shuffled his papers together and limped to the front on his still-sore ankle. "What than I do for you?" he asked, looking straight out at nothing. He took off his glasses and cleaned them, then looked out again and still saw nothing. When he turned to leave, Sherry jumped up and rang the bell again. "Checkin' in!" she shouted.

Four-Eyes turned. "Where are you?"

"Here," she said from below the edge of the counter.

Four-Eyes looked again. "Are you thure you here?"

Sherry was suddenly tired of this game and ran into the kitchen, leaving Four-Eyes scratching his head. Polly had left Cubby and Larry in the kitchen while she ran an errand. The boys were helping Raul, the cook.

Raul looked out into the dining room. He'd filled all the

orders that Ernesto the waiter had brought him and wanted to take a break. Ernesto wanted to go with him.

Raul looked at Cubby and Larry. "Can you two *amigos* handle things while I take a smoke?"

"Shouldn't smoke," said Larry.

Raul grinned. "And you shouldn't mouth off. Can you two handle it for about twenty minutes?"

"Sure!" said Cubby. "No problem!"

The minute Raul and Ernesto were out the door, a burly man came into the dining room and sat down. Larry looked out. "We got trouble now."

Cubby looked out. "Who's goin' to take his order?"

"I will," said Sherry, and started through the swinging kitchen doors.

Cubby grabbed her by the back of her sweater. "Hold it. You need the order pad to write on." He went to Ernesto's station and picked it up. "Here, write his order on this."

Sherry took it, but Larry shook his head. "She can't read or write."

Cubby looked at Sherry. "Just pretend you're writin'. Just scribble, but remember his order so we can fix it up."

They put Ernesto's long white apron around Sherry and pushed her through the doors into the dining room. She tripped on the first step, and then walked like a cowboy, with the long apron trailing between her legs.

Cubby rubbed his hands together and smiled at Larry. "Man, we goin' to get some big tips with our food!"

Larry smiled, but he wasn't so sure as he watched his sister walk as if bowlegged. Sherry approached the man and smiled. "Checkin' in?" she asked. Sherry had never eaten in a hotel restaurant and didn't know what else to ask.

"No, I'm not checkin' in," the burly man in the suit said. "I want to order some food. Say," he said eyeing Sherry, "are you old enough to work here?"

"Old 'nough. Now what do you want to eat?" she asked.

"You got any ham?"

Sherry closed her eyes. "We don't serve pig meat in here."

The man looked back at the menu. "Says ham right here."

Sherry looked him in the eye. "Ham's gone to heaven."

The man looked at Sherry as if she were loco. "What you got on special?"

Sherry couldn't read the menu or the special board, so she just made things up. "We got a special steak and a special fish and a special chicken and a special pie and . . ."

The man shook his head. "Hold it, hold it. I'll have the special chicken. How's it prepared?"

"Cooked," Sherry answered simply.

"I hope it's cooked, but *how* is it cooked?" the man asked.

"Pan-cooked. Yup, it's oven-cooked chicken."

The man sat back, "Which is it? Pan cooked or oven cooked?"

Sherry huffed back. "They put the chicken in a pan and put the pan in the oven."

"Okay, okay, bring it to me with all the trimmin's and a cup of java, mud thick. I hope the chicken's fresh from huntin' and peckin' around."

Sherry rolled her eyes and drew a picture of a chicken and a mud ball. She walked back to the kitchen with the apron trailing behind her.

Cubby pushed the door closed behind her. "Well, what'd he want?"

Sherry looked at the scribbles on her pad. All she could remember was fresh chicken, some kind of wrapping, and mud. "He wants a fresh chicken all wrapped up like a Christmas present and a cup of mud."

"Mud!" Larry exclaimed. "Are you sure?"

"Heard it with my own ears," she said, showing them the scribbles on her pad. She pointed to a scribble line and to the picture of the mud ball. "That there says mud, and this is a mud ball. I wrote it down just like you told me to."

Cubby looked back out at the man. "How fresh does he want his chicken?"

Sherry shrugged. "Said he wants a fresh huntin' and peekin' chicken."

"That fresh!" laughed Cubby.

"And that's strange," said Larry.

"Yeah," agreed Cubby.

While Cubby and Larry went looking for a chicken and some mud, Terry put Farley's last dollar into his pocket. "That's a fun game, Mr. Farley," he said, shaking the dice.

"It wasn't fun for me," Farley said. He stood up to go. "Say, Red, would you spot me a dollar for a drink? I'm powerful thirsty."

"I can get you some water or milk from the kitchen," Terry said, feeling the money in his pocket.

"Naw, I just need a buck for some whisky over at Tippy's."

"Sorry. Pa said never give a man money for whisky. See you later, Mr. Farley," Terry said, skipping away.

While Cubby and Larry were looking for a fresh chicken, Sherry looked into the busboy tray and saw leftover food on some dirty dishes. She scraped it into a bowl with her fingers and found a half-eaten roll. She used her fingers to spread butter all over it and hide the bite marks.

After arranging it on a plate she'd wiped clean with a rag, she took it back out to the man. "Here's some thank you's."

"Thank you's?" he asked.

Sherry smiled. "That's what I always call everythin' passed to me at the table."

"Thanks," he said, taking the strange combination of vegetables, meats, and bread. "What is it?"

"Special," Sherry said. "Try it. You'll like it."

The man took a big spoonful and started to put it in his mouth. "Stop!" screamed Sherry.

"What?" he stammered, spilling the food onto his lap. "What's wrong?"

Sherry shook her head. "You didn't say grace."

"I'm too big for that. Now go on and get out of here," he said, spooning another bite.

"Got to say grace, or you'll be the next one to die." The man stopped the spoon near his open mouth, looked at Sherry, and lowered the spoon. "Look, kid, if you want to say grace for me, great. I'll wait. But I don't have to say it!"

"Okay," Sherry said. "Hold hands." She reached out and took the man's hand. He quickly pulled his hand away, since her hand was covered with butter.

"Sorry," she said, wiping her hands on the apron. "That's better," she said, taking his hand again. "Now let's say grace." She took a deep breath and began singing grace to the tune of the "Star Spangled Banner":

> Oh, God can't you see,
> By the dog's early fight,
> That the food is for you,
> That we're waitin' to eat now,
> Who's broad steak and bright . . .

The man put his hand up. "Hold it. Hold it! That's enough. Time to eat. Get out of here, right now!" he said, turning her around and pushing her back toward the kitchen.

Meanwhile, the great chicken hunt was going on in the shed behind the hotel. Cubby spotted it first. "Aha! Thought so!"

"What?" asked Larry.

"There it is—a fresh chicken!" Cubby pointed to the chicken in the wire pen and dashed to get it.

"Now all we have to do is figure a way to wrap it," Larry mumbled.

Back in the kitchen, Cubby took the chicken and held it squawking in the air, a knife in his other hand. "You kill it," Cubby said, handing the chicken to Larry.

"Not me. You do it," Larry said, handing the squawking chicken right back.

Sherry looked at them both. "Man said fresh wrapped, so I got this from the storage room." She was holding a five-foot length of wrapping paper and some ribbon.

It took them a while to wrap the chicken like a Christmas present, but after they tied its legs together and taped its beak shut, it didn't move. Cubby put the wrapped surprise meal onto the tray with the cup of mud that Larry had made from the mud crust under the snow out back.

"Just what the customer ordered," Cubby said, pushing Sherry through the swinging doors into the dining room.

Sherry walked over to the table and set the tray down. "Here's your fresh chicken with all the wrappin's and a cup of mud," she said proudly.

He eyed the package. "Why's it wrapped?"

She smiled. "Silly! 'Cause it's Christmas!"

The man managed a smile and pulled at the wrapped fresh chicken dinner. He managed to pull the string off the chicken's feet and wings along with the wrapping paper. The chicken flew off with the wrapping and went flying around the room in a sea of feathers.

"What the heck?" he screamed, ducking as the chicken made a pass over his head. He reached to take a quick sip of coffee and spit it out, coughing.

"That's mud!" he screamed.

"That's what you asked for," Sherry said, ducking as the chicken flew past.

The chicken flew overhead and landed on the man's shoulders. He stood up, trying to shake the chicken loose, and ran screaming from the restaurant with the chicken flapping away.

Cubby looked out the front window and saw Polly returning at the same time that Larry looked out the back window and saw Raul and Ernesto coming back. They both threw up their hands and flew through the room, picking up feathers and cleaning up the evidence.

Raul and Ernesto slapped the boys on their backs. "Thanks, *amigos.*" Raul said. "You guys are all right."

Polly looked into the kitchen. "Havin' a good time?"

Sherry beamed. "You wouldn't believe what happened. First I . . ."

Raul whispered, "Cover for us."

Larry clamped his hand over his sister's mouth. "Things have just been fun."

"Yeah," said Cubby, trying to take up the slack. "We pretended we worked in the hotel."

"That's good," said Polly. "Where's Terry?"

Terry skipped into the kitchen. "I'm right here."

"And what have you been doin'?" Polly asked, lowering her head and squinting a bit.

"Oh, just learnin' how to play craps," he said, smiling.

Polly shook her head and wondered what they weren't telling her.

Meanwhile, Kris Kringle was over at the livery, talking horse trading with the blacksmith. Seemed the smithy had taken a liking to his big roan horse and offered him a two-for-one trade.

Kris scratched his chin. "Hm. I guess Uncle Sam won't mind," he said, accepting the deal.

The trade would leave him with an extra horse that just might fit Santa's need list. Now he had Terry's knife and Larry's horse.

"Where am I going to get a pig for Sherry, though?" he asked himself as he walked back toward the hotel. He entered without the children seeing him.

CHAPTER 28

TRAPPED

The air inside the Helling cabin was almost as cold as the blizzard raging around it. Jacob was beside himself as Martha cried and Laura argued with him to let Dr. George help her.

"He's a doctor, you stubborn old mule!" Laura shouted, circling around Jacob. "If it were you in pain, you'd have no problem letting Dr. George help you!"

Jacob turned in a circle, following her movement. "I don't want no . . ." he looked over and saw Dr. George reach forward as Martha Helling cried.

"Keep your cotton-pickin' hands off her!"

Dr. George turned with fiery eyes. "These hands have never picked cotton! I'm a doctor, not some sharecropper who's willin' to let his wife die over his own hatred!"

Jacob started forward, raising his fists. "I'm goin' to teach you a . . ."

Laura grabbed his arm. "One more step and we're leaving."

Jacob's expression changed. "You can't leave, Mrs. Wilder. You're the midwife."

"I'm not a midwife, and if you threaten Dr. George again or call him names, we're leaving—and taking your wife with us."

Martha screamed out in pain. The sheets were red. "She's spotting blood bad, Laura," Dr. George called over. "Get some clean rags and hot water, quick!"

Laura turned to Jacob. "You either help now or go sit in the barn with the rest of the animals. The choice is yours. Which is it?"

The blood stain spread on the sheets and Jacob turned white. "There's sheets in the trunk. I'll make rags and bandages."

Martha's condition was touch and go throughout the day.

Sheriff Peterson stopped by with Rev. Youngun and the Kamarov family. They had stabilized Boris's condition, and were taking his family back to town while there was still time.

Laura stood outside with the sheriff. "Looks like the blizzard's let up."

"You best come back with us now," the sheriff said. "There's a lull in the storm, but it's goin' to get worse."

Laura shook her head. "Can't leave. She's going to deliver that baby any time. She's already spottin' blood, and Dr. George is worried that he might have to do a cesarean."

"She'll die from it unless she's back in the doc's office. You ain't got the proper equipment up here."

Dr. George stepped out to get a bit of fresh air. "The baby's not ready yet. Things couldn't be goin' any worse."

"Can she travel?" Sheriff Peterson asked. "We could be back in town in about an hour if the weather holds up."

Dr. George shook his head. "Her fever's too hot and with the blood and baby the way it is, it'd be too dangerous."

Rev. Youngun got off the sheriff's sleigh and walked over. "Anything I can do to help?" he asked.

"We're about out of firewood, and Jacob won't leave the house to get any," Laura said in a disgusted tone.

"I'll chop some up," Rev. Youngun said, heading off to the barn.

Sheriff Peterson called out after him, "You comin' back with us?"

"We'll be back by nightfall. Right, Doc?" Rev. Youngun called out.

Dr. George rubbed his eyes. "Or sooner."

Sheriff Peterson brushed the snow off his cap. "I best be goin'. Good luck with the baby—and gettin' back to town." He looked up into the sky as the wind picked up. "The blizzard's just let go of the rope to spit on its hand. It's goin' to be back with a vengeance soon."

Laura said, "Stop by Apple Hill and tell Manly I may be home late, will you?"

"No problem. Your place is on the way," Sheriff Peterson said, trudging back to his cutter.

"Tell him I'll be all right and not to worry," she called out after him.

"I'll give him the message; the rest is up to him."

Laura watched them until they were out of sight. A gust of wind picked up her hair. *Blizzard's got it in for us,* she thought, shivering against the numbing cold.

The sheriff's trip back was not an easy one, and the one-hour trip to town turned into a two-hour trip to Apple Hill. He pulled in and knocked on the Wilders' door.

Manly answered. "Sheriff, come on in and take a load off. Want some coffee?"

"We can just stop in and warm up, then I'll get these Russians back to town and leave 'em at Rev. Youngun's church." He carefully stepped down the stairs and said over his shoulder, "Got a message from your wife."

Manly looked out at the huddled immigrants. "Come on in. It's warm in here!"

Sheriff Peterson lifted Boris out and carried him inside. "Light case of frostbite," he said to Manly as he laid Boris by the fireplace. "Found him half-froze to death up near the Hel-lings'."

Manly gave Boris's wife a cup of coffee. "It's hot. Just let him sip," he warned. "What's the message from Laura?" he asked.

"That they couldn't leave Hellings' until the baby comes. Doc said it was bad and gettin' worse. Left Rev. Youngun up there to chop wood."

"They say when they'd get back?" Manly asked with a look of concern on his face.

Sheriff Peterson clicked his tongue and shook his head. "Said by nightfall, but with the mess they're in up there and the blizzard comin' back, I wouldn't be holdin' my breath."

Rose came into the kitchen. "Where's Mother?"

Manly gave her a false smile. "She's still up helpin' to deliver that baby. She'll be back by suppertime."

Long after the sheriff had left and supper had passed, Manly stood on the front porch, shielding his eyes against the raging storm, looking for Laura.

At that same moment, Laura was looking out the cabin win-dow, wishing she was back home. Wishing she was safe, away from the pain, suffering, and hatred that had made the cabin so suffocating.

Then Dr. George cried out, "Laura, come quick!"

By morning, everyone in the cabin was exhausted and Laura was sick and tired of playing Jacob Helling's game and being the doctor's hands. It couldn't go on much longer, and Laura thought about performing a cesarean on the woman. There was just no way. She wasn't up to it. But she was trapped by the weather and trapped by circumstances beyond her control.

CHAPTER 29

THE DAY BEFORE CHRISTMAS

When Rev. Youngun and Dr. George didn't return, Polly took it upon herself to stay the night with Cubby and the three Younguns in the hotel. After a pillow fight that covered the halls with feathers, and plenty of wrestling, they finally calmed down when Four-Eyes Johnson told them that Santa was in the hotel.

"If you thildren don't thalm down, I'll tell Thanta!" Four-Eyes threatened, wagging his finger at them.

"What did you ask Santa to bring you, Mr. Johnson?" Larry asked.

Four-Eyes made a gummy smile. "All I want for Thhrithtmath ith my new teeth."

"We saw Santa at the bridge. Is he really here, Mr. Johnson?" Sherry asked.

"Why, he thure ith, tho you betht be good or you'll get nothin' but thwittheth for Thhrithtmath," Four-Eyes said, closing their door.

"Hey, Mr. Johnson," Larry called out.

"Yeth, thon?" Four-Eyes asked, looking through the crack in the door.

"Can we see Santa tomorrow?" Larry asked.

"He'th a buthy man, tho I wouldn't dithturb him. Good night," he said, closing the door.

"Is he really in the hotel, Miss Polly?" Terry asked, tugging her robe.

"That's what I heard. Now you children best be gettin' to sleep."

"Ain't no Santa Claus," Cubby grumbled.

"Is too!" Larry said. "We saw him at the Willow Creek Bridge!"

"Did not! It's just a white folks' dream, ain't it, Miss Polly?" Cubby asked, looking to her for support.

"Santa's for everyone, Cubby. His love is color-blind," Polly said with a warm smile.

"And Mr. Springer said he was part black, although he didn't really look it," said Sherry matter-of-factly.

Polly looked over and shook her head in amazement. She never knew what to expect from the Youngun kids. "What did Mr. Springer say?"

Larry said, "Santa could be part black or all black. White artists just draw him white because they are."

Terry spoke up. "Said Santa's middle name is Lemuel, and that there ain't no white man with the name of Lemuel. It's a black name."

"I never heard that," said Cubby. "Only pictures I ever saw of Santa was a big white man in a red suit." He shook his head. "I think it's all baloney."

"If Mr. Springer said it, it's true!" Sherry screamed.

"Children. Children!" Polly said, waving her hands up and down for quiet. "Santa's a man of all colors. Now let's get to sleep."

Terry started crying. "Think Pa's okay?"

Cubby looked up from under the covers. "And Pops?"

Polly tucked them all in. "They'll be back here tomorrow, don't you worry." She turned off the light and said in the dark, "Good night, children."

By morning, the main street was a sight to see—if you could see it. Snowdrifts were piled as high as the second stories of the shops and houses. The sheriff and his helpers had to dig passageways to the front doors of some homes, so the people could get out.

Fuel supplies ran low, and people resorted to burning green wood, furniture, hay, and anything that seemed flammable. The churches' temporary shelters were filled.

Sheriff Peterson had to climb up on the roof of Granny Hoban's house to get her out, but he fell off the roof and fractured his arm. Father Walsh set his arm and left the sheriff in the hotel to wait while he and the strong lads from the Hardacres carried out the sheriff's duties.

Manly had been up all night, worrying about Laura, and in the morning he put out plenty of food in the barn and locked it tight. He took Rose into town to stay at the hotel, planning to get the sheriff and bring Laura back.

Manly walked back into the hotel lobby after leaving Rose with Polly and the kids. When he saw the sheriff sitting in the corner with his arm in a sling and his feet propped up, a look of disappointment crossed his face. "What happened to you?"

The sheriff shook his head. "I fell off Granny Hoban's roof and broke my durn arm."

"I was comin' to get you to go with me up to the Hellings' and bring Laura and the rest back," Manly said, sitting down beside him.

The sheriff grinned weakly. "I wouldn't be much good to you. Can't even drive a sleigh with this arm."

"What am I goin' to do?" Manly said, shaking his head.

Edwin Ebenezer, the crotchety old veteran, was playing cards with Farley over in the corner. Farley was trying to win back some of the money he'd lost to Terry.

Edwin heard Manly and said loudly, "God hates a coward, Manly. It you want to save them, see if God wants you to do it."

Manly looked over. "Edwin, you better hope that God don't have it in for mean old men, or you'll wish for this blizzard where you'll be goin'."

Farley whistled. "Them's fightin' words if I ever heard 'em."

Sheriff Peterson patted Manly on the arm. "Don't let him rub you wrong. He's just an ol' cuss."

Edwin cackled. "I might be old, but if it were my woman up there, I'd have already been up there and got her."

Manly stood up. "I need to cool off." He limped past Edwin and Farley and left them cackling as he walked out into the cold. The blizzard appeared to be letting up. There was really no decision for Manly to make; he was going to go get Laura.

After telling Rose his plans, Manly packed his cutter with food, matches, an axe, rope, lantern, and whatever supplies he could find in the hotel's storeroom. He grabbed a half-dozen blankets and found an old buffalo robe to wrap around himself.

Sheriff Peterson watched him glumly. "My arm might be hurt, but I could still go along to help guide you."

Manly cinched the supplies onto the back. "If somethin' happens, I wouldn't be able to save us both. I wish you were comin', but you've got to stay here."

Sheriff Peterson looked through the thinning snow in the air. "The blizzard's lettin' up, but it's a tricky one, it is. Run straight and fast. Ten people've died in the county so far. We don't need you to be number eleven."

Manly wrapped the buffalo robe firmly around him. "I don't intend to die. I'm not the hero type."

"Don't kid yourself, Manly. What you're doin' takes more guts than you know," Peterson said, patting Manly on the back.

Manly set out in the cutter, waving to Peterson. The jingling bells on the cutter made a Christmas sound as he went down the center of Main Street. Rose looked out from a second-floor window as her father's team pulled the cutter out of sight.

CHAPTER 30

A DAY OF WAITING

The lull in the weather lasted less than twenty minutes. Soon Manly found himself being whipsawed back and forth by the blinding winds. The snow cut his face like pieces of glass, and once again he had to cover the horses' eyes.

With the deep snow and blinding conditions, it was hard to distinguish the road from the fields. Once across the Willow Creek Bridge, the road was just a guessing game.

Several times Manly found himself up dead ends or dangling on the edge of a sharp cliff. What kept him going on, exhausted and snowblind, were guts, sheer determination, and his undying love for Laura.

His destination was just a few miles up the road, but under the conditions, it seemed like the end of the earth. Every step was a struggle for the horses. Each time the runners froze in place, Manly thought his heart would give out as he pushed with everything he had.

In the Helling cabin a few miles away, tension filled the air. Dr. George peered at the movement Laura was pointing out in Martha's stomach.

Laura asked Dr. George, "Think it could be twins?"

Dr. George looked at the movement on both sides of Martha's stomach. "Feel over there." Laura's fingers moved across Martha's stomach. "Feel the same thing?"

Laura nodded. "Feels like four feet to me."

"Twins?" Jacob was astonished. "She's goin' to have twins?" He sat down quickly, with a look of utter bewilderment on his face.

Dr. George shook his head. "Don't know, but I think so. What it means is double trouble." He looked at Rev. Youngun. "We need to get this woman back to my office."

Laura stood up and looked down at Martha. "I don't think we'd make it."

When Martha awoke, Dr. George patted her arm. "I think your two children are about ready to enter the world."

"Two? You said two babies?" Martha asked weakly.

Dr. George took a towel and wiped the perspiration from her face. "You waited this long to have a baby, so you're gettin' a bonus."

Rev. Youngun stood by the bed. "You're holdin' up well, Martha."

"Where are your kids, Preacher?" Martha asked weakly.

"They're at the Mansfield Hotel with Polly. I hope everything's all right."

Dr. George laughed. "I'm sure Polly's got everythin' under control."

At that exact moment, Four-Eyes was walking the floors, doing his rounds, when he saw a huge, white shape up ahead, getting bigger by the moment.

"Help! Raul, Ernesto, help!" he screamed, backing away.

Raul, in the kitchen, looked up when he heard his name called. "Hey, Ernesto, did you hear that?"

Ernesto nodded. "Sounded like Old Man Johnson callin' you."

"Oh, man," Raul said, taking off his apron. "What does he want now?"

Polly was knitting in her room after making Christmas fudge with the children. She had been worried that the children wouldn't have anything for Christmas morning. She wanted them to at least have the fudge treats wrapped in colorful paper.

It had been hard getting the kids not to eat the mixture before she baked it, but after smacking a few hands with her spatula, she'd gotten their attention. By mid-afternoon, it smelled so good in the kitchen that Terry was half-crazed by the wait.

Polly gave them each one candy, wrapped up the rest, and put them in the kitchen cupboard until Christmas morning. While she knitted, the three boys played cards. Terry taught the others to play a card-counting game that Farley had taught him.

"Is it a nice game?" Polly asked, not looking up from her knitting.

"Yes, ma'am," Terry said. "This countin' game makes you good at math. It's like doin' homework."

"That's good," Polly said, clicking her needles contentedly.

"No, no, no!" said Terry as Cubby put down two kings and a five. "You can only go up to twenty-one. You got twenty-five."

"But twenty-five is more than twenty-one," Cubby protested.

"But Larry got fifteen and I got nineteen, which is closer to twenty-one, so I win," Terry said, collecting three nickels. "Got any more money, boys?" he asked with a grin on his face.

Suddenly, they heard Four-Eyes screaming. Polly dropped her knitting and stepped quickly toward the door. Four-Eyes fell into the room, shaking all over. His glasses fell onto the rug.

"What's wrong, Mr. Johnson?" Polly asked.

Four-Eyes picked up his glasses and looked at her. "Blondie! Oh, I'm tho glad to thee you, Blondie!" He jumped back up on his feet. "Look down the hall. Do you thee the thnow monthter?"

"Thnow monthter?" Terry repeated. "What'th that?"

Polly gave Terry a disapproving look, then peered carefully around the corner. What she saw took her breath away. It was the largest mass of soap bubbles she'd ever seen—and it was getting bigger.

Polly looked around the room. "Where's Sherry?" she asked the boys.

Larry looked up. "She's down the hall takin' a bath."

"Yeah," said Terry, making a face and wiggling his arms around. "A girlie bubble bath."

Raul stood at the doorway, staring at the ever-growing mass of soap bubbles. *"Ay caramba!* What is that, Mr. Johnson?"

"It'th a . . ." Four-Eyes stumbled for words.

"What is it, Polly?" Raul asked.

Polly shook her head. "It's a bubble bath gone wild, I think."

Inside the bathroom, Sherry had emptied the entire box of soap into the tub and kept the drain open so she could keep the water running. When the hot water started coming, she laid back like the Queen of Sheba in a mountain of soap bubbles.

She hadn't even noticed that the bubbles had overflowed the tub and were making their way down the hall. But she did hear Polly calling her name.

"I'm in here, Miss Polly," she shouted back.

Polly turned to the three boys. "Can one of you get through this soapy mess and turn off the water?"

"I can!" they all shouted in unison.

"Let 'em all go," suggested Raul. "They all could use a bath."

The three boys waded down the hallway. Larry got to the tub first and turned the water off.

"Hey!" Sherry screamed. "Who did that?"

"Me," said Larry, who was covered with bubbles.

"Are you a boy?" Sherry asked, covering herself.

"I'm your brother Larry," he said, brushing the bubbles from his face.

"Get out. Get out!" she screamed, and began throwing soap bars and scrub brushes. Larry ducked them, but they disappeared into the soapy unknown, hitting Terry and Cubby.

If it hadn't been for Polly emerging through the bubbles at that exact moment, a fight would have broken out. She picked up Sherry from the bath, wrapped a towel around her, and marched straight back through the bubbles toward her room.

Four-Eyes was startled when Polly walked out of the soap mess. Polly's black hair was covered with a mound of white bubbles that stood three feet high. Four-Eyes frowned, "Blondie, why'd you tholor your hair?"

Polly shook white bubbles from her head as she passed Raul. "You better get movin'. These bubbles will ruin the wallpaper if they stay on too long."

Polly set Sherry on the bed and finger-combed the last white soap bubbles out of her own thick, black hair. Four-Eyes smiled. "That'th better, now you're my thweet blonde Blondie again."

Raul rolled his eyes, "Mr. Johnson, you need to get your glasses checked."

Four-Eyes pulled off his glasses and looked at them. "Funny, that'th what everyone thayth."

CHAPTER 31

COUNTDOWN

"Push, Martha. Push!" Dr. George urged.

"What if the baby doesn't come soon?" Laura whispered.

Dr. George rubbed his eyes. "Then we'll have to operate."

"Here, Doc," Rev. Youngun said, handing him clean sheets.

"Thanks. We'll need your prayers soon, preacherman." Dr. George looked at Laura. "We'll need everyone's prayers."

Laura shivered. "This place is cold. We need more heat."

"I'm tryin' the best I can," said Rev. Youngun.

Dr. George looked at Jacob, who was staring aimlessly out the window. "Jacob, we need your help. Get to the barn and bring in more wood."

Jacob turned, a blank look in his eyes. "All we got left is hay."

Laura glared. "Then make more prairie logs! Go bring in enough hay to keep this place warm!"

Dr. George looked at Rev. Youngun. "Go break up the table and chairs and put 'em in the fireplace. I'm goin' to need your help here soon, when we start to cut."

A look of relief swept over Laura's face. "I'm glad you said 'we'."

Dr. George handed her the scalpel. "I'll be watchin' your every move."

Just down the hill, within sight of the smoke from the chimney, was Manly. But with the driving snow, he could hardly see his lead horse. He had no idea how close he was.

Manly pushed as hard as he could, but the cutter wouldn't budge. When it had slipped off the road into the drift, the runners had gotten hooked by a branch.

The snow was falling faster than he could dig, and it seemed a hopeless task. He pushed again and for a moment thought he had the sleigh free. It jolted forward, pulling him off his feet. A branch cracked in front of the horses and scared them backward, pinning Manly against the snowbank.

He tried to push the sleigh off, but he just sank deeper into the snowbank. The storm broke momentarily, and for the first time, he saw the smoke from the cabin, just ahead.

"Help! Help!" he screamed.

Jacob Helling was standing outside and thought he heard a voice. He looked around, but figured it was the storm playing tricks on his mind.

Manly struggled to get out and screamed again. "Help me, I'm stuck!"

The storm whipped up again, and Manly watched helplessly as Jacob trudged off to the barn. His words were lost in the thick blanket of snow that covered everything and was getting thicker by the moment.

Manly sat like a man trapped in quicksand, looking for something to save him, with only his buffalo robe to protect him from the deadly cold.

CHAPTER 32

ARE YOU SANTA?

Larry, Terry, and Cubby spent the rest of the afternoon searching for Santa. They peeked around every corner and hid in the stairwells, looking for the man in red.

Sherry took a different approach. She got a plate of cookies from Raul and asked, "What room is Santa in?"

"Santa? You mean Santa Claus?" Raul asked.

"You know," Sherry said coyly.

Ernesto was listening. "You mean the big heavy guy with the long white hair? The mailman?"

"Yeah," said Sherry, thinking about Santa taking their letters on the Willow Creek Bridge, "the mailman."

"He's in room two-o-four."

"Thanks," said Sherry, heading toward the stairs with the cookies.

Sherry looked at the room numbers and finally saw a two, zero, and four together. Her face brightened as she knocked.

"Who is it?" came a muffled, sleepy voice.

"It's me—Sherry—Santa. I've got some cookies for you."

Kris Kringle was snug under the covers and didn't want to be disturbed. "Come back later. I'm sleeping up for my big run tonight."

Sherry knocked again. "I won't bother you. I'll just leave the chocolate cookies in front of the door."

Sherry put the cookies down and hid by the door. Kris wiggled his nose, thinking about the cookies, and got out of bed in his red long johns. He carefully unlocked the door and reached down for the cookies.

"Santa!" Sherry screamed. "I love you, Santa!"

"I love you too, little girl." He unhooked her from his leg. "Now you run along so I can get dressed. Got lots of toys to deliver tonight."

"But, Santa," she cried out, latching onto his leg again.

Just at that moment, Rose was walking down the hallway. "Kris! It's me, Rose, Rose Wilder." She gave him a big bear hug. "I didn't know you were back."

"You invited me to Apple Hill Farm for Christmas. I've just been waitin' for the snow to let up." He tried to take a step but felt a weight on his leg and looked down. Sherry Youngun was wrapped tightly around him. He managed to walk into the room, dragging the burdened leg behind.

Larry and Terry came stumbling into the room. "It's Santa!" they both said in unison. Cubby hung back at the doorway, staring.

Rose laughed. "They love you, Santa."

Kris shook his head and sat on the chair next to the writing desk. He took out the Younguns' letters. "You each wanted some mighty hard gifts to find," he said, looking at them all, "so I need to keep working on it. You better run on now, so I can zip up to the North Pole and get my toy bag."

He saw Cubby peering in. "Come on in, young man. Have you written to Santa yet?"

"No, and I'm not goin' to," Cubby said, and ran down the hall.

"What's wrong with him?" Santa asked.

Larry frowned. "He doesn't believe in Santa. All he wants for Christmas is his momma back."

"Where's his momma?" Santa asked.

"She's dead. She's in heaven with my Bessie and my momma," Sherry said, a tear in her eye.

"Well, Santa can't change some things, but I'm sure he'll bring something for that little boy," Kris said.

Cubby came back in. "I know my momma's dead," he said, "but I want my new Pops back. I love him."

Kris saw Rose turn her face. "And what do you want for Christmas, Rose Wilder?"

Rose turned. "I want my mother and father back safely. They're somewhere out there," she said, pointing to the blizzard outside. "They're out there with his Pops and their father," she said, pointing to the three sad-faced Youngun children.

"Santa will bring them back," Sherry sniffed. "Santa can do anything. I want my daddy back."

Santa's only human, Kris thought.

Out in the shadows, covered over with snow, Manly watched the second horse fall over. Now two had frozen to death. The other two horses struggled under the reins, trying to free themselves, but they were trapped like Manly.

He fought to stay awake, but the numbing cold was enveloping him, urging him to sleep forever.

CHAPTER 33

CHRISTMAS EVE

As dusk set in, the storm was still raging. It was a gloomy Christmas Eve in Mansfield, as word filtered out that Dr. George, Laura, and Rev. Youngun were trapped in the Hellings' cabin and Manly had gone out in the blizzard to save them.

Father Walsh and Rev. Moses led the people in the hotel's dining room in prayer for the town and those in danger. Cubby was wrapped in Polly's arms, sick with worry about his pops. The three Youngun children sat together, realizing for the first time that they might lose their father. Their mother was buried in the town cemetery. What would they do without their father? Who would take them in?

No one noticed as Kris Kringle snuck down the back stairs in his red stocking cap. He slipped out the side door, his sounds covered by the noise of new arrivals coming into the hotel lobby and stomping their feet. A rush of cold air swept through the dining room.

Maurice and Eulla Mae Springer and their cousin Lemuel came into the room, brushing snow off their coats. Lemuel winked at Rose, who waved back.

Father Walsh nodded to the new arrivals. "You're all welcome here. We're prayin' for the storm to let up and . . ."

Maurice declared, "It's all Christmas colors out there."

"It's what?" Father Walsh asked.

"It's one big Christmas tree in the sky," Maurice said. "Go look. It just started."

Everyone in the room crowded by the dining room windows to look at the northern lights. The storm had subsided, and there were ripples of red, green, and yellow waving across the sky, mixed with a pinkish haze in the background.

"Santa's coming!" Sherry screamed out.

Lemuel Springer leaned over and whispered to Rose, "Bells of glory brought us Santa to the train, didn't it, girl?"

Rose smiled. "I'll believe in Santa Claus. I just hope my parents are safe."

Father Walsh turned to Rev. Moses. "Let's gather up all the children and tell them the Christmas story."

Miles away, across the hills, a baby was trying to be born.

Dr. George walked over to Jacob. "Your wife may die, and the death will be on your hands."

"She's in God's hands." said Jacob.

"Well, I'll tell you what. I'll put you in God's hands and see how you like it."

"What? What are you talkin' 'bout?"

Dr. George took Jacob by the collar and seat of his pants and lifted him toward the door. "I'm goin' to put your sorry tail out the door and see how you do."

Jacob fought and struggled, but Dr. George held strong. When he opened the door, a blast of cold air whipped through the room. Jacob screamed, "But I'll die out there in the cold! You can't do that!"

"Watch me!" Dr. George said. "It doesn't have to be this way. Just like your wife doesn't have to die because of your hatred and ignorance!"

"But, but . . ." Jacob stammered.

"Aint no buts 'bout it, but you're goin' out into the deep freeze." He tossed Jacob out into the cold and slammed the door shut, latching it.

While Jacob hammered against the door with his fists, Dr. George took a drink of coffee and sat back down next to Laura. She grinned. "That's some bedside manner you have, Doc."

"An old professor at med school told us, off the record, that sometimes you have to do what you have to do to save a life."

Laura looked at Dr. George. "What are we going to do? The baby won't come out."

Jacob beat against the door. "Let me in! Let me in!"

Dr. George grinned, wiping the perspiration from his brow. "We got to operate, ain't no choice." He turned to Rev. Youngun. "Get the water boilin' and get ready to help."

"What about Jacob?" Rev. Youngun asked.

"Open the peek hole and ask him if he's ready to be reasonable."

Rev. Youngun opened the hole. Jacob stuck his face to the two-inch square and begged, "Pl . . . pl . . . pl . . . please let me in. I'm fr . . . fr . . . freezin' to death!"

"Choice is yours," Rev. Youngun said. "Doc needs to operate, and you're bein' a stubborn old cuss. You're in God's hands. You'll be all right," he said, closing the hole.

Jacob stuck his fingers into the hole to keep it from closing. "I'll die out here . . . please."

"And your wife's goin' to die in here," Rev. Youngun answered. "What's it goin' to be?"

"Let me in! He can operate, just let me in!"

Rev. Youngun opened the door, and Jacob fell into the room. His teeth were chattering so hard that he couldn't speak. As Rev. Youngun closed the door, he thought he heard a scream for help. He stepped out into the cold and looked out across the skies lit up by the northern lights.

From down below, Manly saw the cabin lights and the sky

ablaze with colors. It gave him a second round of strength and hope as he cried out, "Help! Help, I'm stuck!"

Rev. Youngun again heard the shouts from somewhere outside the circle of the cabin's light. Was the wind playing tricks with his mind? Then he heard it once more.

"Someone's out there callin' for help!" he said to Dr. George. "I'm goin' to take a look."

"Don't be gone long," Dr. George said. "I'm 'bout ready to start." He turned to Jacob. "Get that fire goin'. Now!" he barked.

Jacob began wrapping prairie logs and stuffing them into the fireplace. The flames rose, sending an enormous heat wave through the room.

"Doc, I think the baby's turning around!" Laura cried out.

"Let me see!" Dr. George said, bending over. "You're right! Boy, we needed this break!"

Rev. Youngun worked his way to the edge of the farm clearing and looked down the drive. The northern lights cast intermittent patches of multicolored light over the leafless trees. He heard the screams again and searched the night shadows.

Manly could see him. "I'm here! I'm stuck down here!" He pushed against the sleigh.

Rev. Youngun saw the two horses still standing and stepped through the deep snow. "Manly?" he shouted. "Is that you, Manly?"

"Yes, it's me! I'm stuck, can't get out!"

Rev. Youngun dug in with his hands, but it was no use.

"Cut the horses off," whispered Manly through his ice-crusted lips.

"What?" asked Rev. Youngun.

"Cut the dead horses off. Push against the sleigh," Manly said weakly.

Rev. Youngun cut the frozen horses loose and dug a path with his hands for the other two horses to follow. He wedged himself between the snowbank and the sleigh and shouted, "Pull! Pull!"

The two horses strained. Rev. Youngun thought his heart would burst as he pushed with all his strength. Finally the runners slowly cracked loose. When the horses inched the cutter a few feet forward, Rev. Youngun pulled Manly out. The second he was free, the sleigh slipped back even further into the snowbank.

"Is Laura all right?" asked Manly, holding onto Rev. Youngun's arm.

"She's inside, deliverin' the baby," Rev. Youngun smiled. "Let's get you into the cabin and the horses into the barn."

"Oh, no!" Manly moaned. "Look!" he said, pointing toward the cabin. Flames were gushing from the top of the mud-and-wood chimney. It looked like a smokestack ablaze.

Inside, Jacob was working like a machine, stoking the fire with hay. He was in such a dazed state that he didn't see the flames licking back down the chimney as the heat lifted the half-burning hay up into the blocked chimney.

Dr. George sighed. "He's comin' out."

"He?" asked Laura, blowing her hair from her eyes.

"Look," he grinned, as the baby appeared. "Looks like a boy to me!" Dr. George took the baby, held him up by his feet, and smacked his fanny lightly. The baby let out a healthy wail. "Sounds just like his father," he grinned, handing the baby to Laura. "Oh, oh, here comes number two," he said, seeing the second baby's head trying to emerge.

Laura took the baby, used warm rags to wipe it off, and handed the small boy to Martha. Dr. George eased the next baby out and started wiping him clean. He turned to Jacob. "You got two sons, Jacob."

Dr. George saw the flames backing down the chimney and poking through the mud-and-wood-slabbed chimney above the mantle. "You're goin' to burn the cabin down! Stop feeding it!"

Jacob turned as a large wrapped piece of burning hay, unable to go up the chimney, floated out from the fireplace. It landed in the haypile in the corner, bursting instantly into flames.

Laura screamed, "Get her out—get her out of here!"

She grabbed Martha by the arm and lifted her up. Martha moaned.

Laura kept her moving forward, saying, "I know it hurts, but you'll die in here. Come on, Martha, we got to get out!"

The two babies were on the bed behind her, and in the confusion of trying to get Martha out, they left the babies inside. Manly and Rev. Youngun came through the door and helped drag Martha and Jacob from the burning cabin.

"Oh no, the babies!" Laura cried, dashing back into the flames before anyone could stop her. She fought through the smoke, tongues of flames darting all around her, and scooped the babies from the bed. She turned to run back out, but a beam from the burning ceiling crashed in front of her.

Manly shouted, "Laura. Laura!"

When Laura screamed as the beam fell, Manly stepped into the burning inferno. He pulled the buffalo robe that was still around his shoulders up over his head and fought his way through the flames.

He stepped over the burning debris and pulled Laura and the two babies under the robe with him, then worked his way to the front door. As they emerged into the brisk cold, Rev. Youngun slapped at the fires that had broken out on parts of the buffalo robe.

"Thank you, Lord," Rev. Youngun said.

"Oh, Manly," Laura said, holding the babies and nuzzling against his chest, "I was so scared."

Jacob started screaming, "The barn! The barn!"

Flames from the house were licking across the connecting shed to the barn. The sleigh horses inside were trying to get out, kicking against the walls.

"We've got to save the sleigh," Dr. George said, "or we'll all die out here."

Laura wrapped the buffalo robe around Martha and laid her on the ground with her two babies while the men raced through the snow toward the barn. They pulled the sleigh outside and went back in for the horses as the roof of the barn went up in a fiery blaze.

Jacob managed to get the horses out, along with the sleigh reins that were on the rail. The pigs were squealing in fright, and the lambs were bleating, but the fire was too fast.

The men lifted Martha into the sleigh and watched the barn go up in flames. The smell of burning animal flesh was thick in the air.

Manly hitched the four horses they'd saved alongside his two and loaded everyone aboard. He looked at Rev. Youngun and said, "You and I will hang onto the back runners. I'm afraid there's too much weight aboard."

"I'll take the reins," Dr. George said. "Laura, you help keep the babies warm."

A squeal caught their attention. A lone piglet with a singed tail came galloping toward them through the snow.

Rev. Youngun scooped up the piglet and smiled. "Laura, would you hold onto this wiggly thing? I think I know a little girl who'd like it, and Jacob will agree it's a fair trade for two healthy sons."

CHAPTER 34

LITTLE HEROES

"Sh. Don't wake Sherry," Larry whispered to his brother.

"Wha . . . what?" Terry stammered, half awake.

"It's time to go," Larry said.

Larry, Terry, and Cubby had a plan to rescue Pops and Pa. After the impromptu service in the hotel dining room, they'd told everyone they wanted to go to sleep early, because Santa was coming in the morning.

Polly had tucked the three boys into the double bed together, not noticing that they had their winter clothes on under their nightshirts. While they waited for Sherry to go to sleep, they decided on their plan. All they knew was that their fathers were stuck up on the back-county hill and that they were going to save them.

While Larry wrote a note, Terry sneaked down into the kitchen to get some provisions. "Get some good food," Larry said.

"Yeah, like mountain men eat," whispered Cubby.

Terry knew exactly what kind of food to get, a food that

would keep them happy, hearty, and strong—a food that tasted better than anything else on earth.

Fudge.

When he got to the kitchen, he went to the cupboard and took out Polly's fudge tray. He opened one of the wrapped Christmas treats and put the whole square into his mouth.

"Just to test it. See if it's poison," he whispered.

He was bound and determined to fill every pocket with the fudge and not leave anything behind. But there were six more pieces left after he'd filled his two jacket pockets and four pants pockets, so he put the rest of the fudge packs into his under-britches.

The note Larry had written said:

Deer Polly,
We have gun to save Pa and Pops. Be back before Santa comes.
Larry

Polly was downstairs with the assembled people, wondering what was happening to Manly and the rest of their good neighbors. The Younguns and Cubby went down the hotel's back stairs and headed out to the barn.

Dangit wiggled to get out of his wooden cage, but Larry shook his head. "Can't take you on this trip, boy. Too dangerous."

They hitched Crab Apple to their sled and took the back alley out of town, listening to Dangit howl his disappointment.

While the northern lights danced overhead, Terry sang quietly, "Better not go where the huskies go and you better not eat the yellow snow."

Larry bopped him on the head. "Be quiet!"

Terry stuck his tongue out. "I hope you know where you're goin'!"

Larry nodded he did, and Terry sat on the back of the sleigh, holding onto Cubby and eating the fudge as fast as he could. Behind them was a trail of wrapping paper, glistening in the Christmas lights flashing in the sky.

They hadn't gotten more than a quarter-mile out of town, when Larry stopped. "What's wrong?" Cubby asked.

"I think we're lost," Larry said. "Can't recognize anything in all this snow."

The wind whipped around them, blinding them with icy particles picked up from the snow's crust. Larry tightened his coat, and Cubby pulled his hat down around his ears.

Terry was eating too fast to think about the cold. "Ithinit'sthaway," Terry mumbled through a mouth full of fudge.

"What'd he say?" Cubby asked.

"What cha eatin'?" Larry asked.

Terry opened a mouth filled with a dark, gooey mass, "I'meatin'Polly'sfudge."

"I can't understand you!" Larry snapped.

Terry gulped. "I said, I'm eatin' Polly's fudge."

"Is that what you brought for food?" Larry asked. "Just fudge?"

"Fudge? Give me some!" Cubby shouted.

Terry handed them each a piece and popped another one in his mouth. Larry guided Crab Apple up the hill toward the hayfield. The temperature dropped as they pulled up the hill.

It was an eerie ride through the glistening haystacks, with the northern lights tossing colors all around. Terry, nodding from the cold, abruptly slipped off the sled.

The sudden snow bath awakened him, and he called out for them to stop. Larry turned and saw that Cubby was asleep against his back. Terry was trudging behind them, the snow above his knees.

Larry looked at the haystacks and said, "Let's dig into this haystack. It'll give us a chance to warm up."

Back at the hotel, Polly went up to check on the children and pulled the blanket carefully over Sherry. She looked over at the bed where the three boys were supposed to be sleeping and saw three shapes under the covers.

She reached over to pull the blanket down a bit, so they could breathe, and saw there were only pillows under the quilt. Then she saw the note by the bed and ran down to the dining room in a panic.

"Maurice! Maurice!" she cried out as she entered the dining room. "They gone!"

"Whoa, girl!" Maurice said, standing up and grabbing her. "Who's gone?"

"The children—Larry, Terry, and Cubby! They've gone after their poppas! Left a note." Maurice read it, shaking his head.

"Them boys want to be little heroes, but if someone don't go find 'em, they'll turn into little icicles out there," Maurice said. The storm rattled the windows.

"Who's gonna find 'em?" Eulla Mae said, shaking her head. "Just you, Lemuel, Mr. Johnson, and the sheriff 'round here right now." Eulla Mae looked around. "Lemuel's too old, and . . ."

Lemuel protested, "I am not. I'm . . ."

Eulla Mae interrupted him. "Hush, old man, you'd freeze your skinny old hide off out there." She looked over at Four-Eyes. "Mr. Johnson can't see well enough to find the front door, and sheriff's got himself a hurt arm." She looked at her husband. "That leaves just you."

"And me," Kris Kringle said, walking into the room.

"Santa can save them," Lemuel said. "He saved my skinny old self, and he can save those chillens."

Maurice sighed. "Who are you?"

Lemuel answered for him. "I told you, this is Kris Krinkle Claus."

Kris stuck out his hand. "My name is Kris Kringle, and I'll come with you."

"You got a sleigh?" Maurice asked.

"Does Santa got a sleigh?" Lemuel exclaimed. " 'Course he got a sleigh. It was made at the North Pole, it was."

Maurice closed his eyes for a moment, then said quietly, "Okay, Lemuel. Maybe you need some sleep." He looked at Kris and said, "Santa, if you're ready, we best be goin'. Those kids could be freezin' to death before you know it."

Raul stuck his head through the kitchen door. "Miss Polly, someone took all your Christmas fudge."

Out in the barn, while Maurice and Kris hitched up the sleigh, Dangit fought to get out of his cage.

Kris looked over. "That dog is crazy to get out."

"Dangit," Maurice said without explaining.

"Did you hurt yourself?" Kris asked.

" 'Scuse me?" Maurice said.

"You said 'dangit.' I was just . . ."

Maurice laughed. "Oh, Dangit's that fool dog's name. He belongs to them three Youngun kids."

"Let him loose. We'll follow him," Kris said. Maurice let the dog loose, and Dangit went yipping up the alley. Kris watched him run. "Think he's following their trail?"

"No doubt about it," Maurice grinned, pointing to the trail of fudge wrappers leading out of town.

The jingling sleigh bells sang with each step of the horses as they pulled down the alley, following the wrappers.

The three boys had taken refuge from the cold by digging into a huge haystack. They'd dug enough room to bring in Crab Apple the mule, and they were temporarily snug, away from the cold winds blowing outside their shelter.

"How's Santa goin' to find us in here?" Terry moaned.

"Santa knows where we are," Larry answered, feeling the cold numb his arms.

"You still believe in that white Santa?" Cubby asked scornfully.

"White or black, it don't matter to me," Terry sighed, closing his eyes, "as long as he's got what I want, he could be polka-dot for all I care."

"I'd like a cup of hot chocolate, right now," Cubby said, hugging himself. "Yeah, that and some pork chop soup."

"Pork chop soup?" Terry said, half-asleep. "You eat that?"

"You never had pork chop soup? It's good."

"I'd like some fudge," said Larry. "Got any more?"

Terry reached into his pants and brought out a warm, squishy wrapped piece. "Here!" he said proudly.

Larry looked at the soggy mess and frowned. Cubby laughed, "I wouldn't eat that if I was dyin'!"

Crab Apple ate the underbritches fudge and even chewed on the wrapper.

As the haystack got colder and colder, Larry did his best to keep them awake. When Terry drifted off to sleep because it was way past his bedtime, Cubby and Larry tried to keep awake, playing number games and rock-scissors-paper with their fists. It was a little hard to play in the dark, so they did it on the honor system, which didn't work out all that well.

"Do you know any good stories?" Cubby asked.

"I know a Christmas story," Larry said in the dark.

"I'm gonna get comfortable as I can. It's gettin' cold in here."

Larry began, "Well, it was the night before Christmas, and all through the farm, not a creature was stirring inside the barn. And Dangit in his basket and Pa in his cap, had just settled down for a good night's nap, when . . ."

They both drifted off halfway through the story, numbed by the cold.

The cold whipped up the snow around them as Kris and Maurice slowly followed the trail of wrappers outside town and around in circles.

"They must have gotten lost," Maurice said.

As Dangit yipped ahead, the snowstorm came back, covering the wrapper trail. "We got to move fast," said Maurice, "or we'll never be able to find them."

Kris snapped the reins, and they drove up through the hayfields outside of town. The snow was so heavy that Maurice's hair and face were frozen white.

The temperature had dropped rapidly inside the haystack. Only the warmth that Crab Apple generated kept the boys alive.

Larry faintly heard the sleigh bells and opened his eyes. "Do you hear it?" he asked, shaking Cubby. Cubby's lips were blue from the cold. "Cubby, wake up!"

Cubby opened his eyes. "I'm so cold," he whispered.

Larry shook Terry awake. "We've got to keep awake, or we'll die!" He cocked his head again at the sound of the bells. "Don't you hear it? Don't you hear the bells?"

Terry's eyes half opened. "It's Santa," he whispered through his icy lips. "Santa's comin'."

"Don't believe," Cubby mumbled. "Don't believe in no Santa."

Neither Cubby nor Terry could keep their eyes open. The numbing sleep was calling them to drift away into the peaceful sleep of a frozen death. Larry was tired, dead tired, but he fought to keep awake.

Suddenly Maurice saw Dangit sitting beside a haystack where Crab Apple's tail and back legs stuck out. "Bet they're in there," he said, pointing it out to Kris.

They pulled the sleigh up next to the stack, and Kris got off. He parted the hay and looked inside.

Larry's eyes went wide. "Santa!" he mumbled.

"Ho ho ho!" Kris laughed. "Time for Santa to get you home."

Terry opened his eyes. "I knew you'd come, Santa. I knew you'd come," he mumbled, drifting back to sleep.

Kris pulled his head out of the haystack and said to Maurice, "They're in there, all right."

"Let me see," Maurice said, bending down.

Maurice stuck his head into the center; right into Cubby's face, sending a pile of hay over Larry, blocking his view. The hay made Larry feel very sleepy, and he nodded off, thinking that Santa had come to save them.

Cubby's eyes popped open. With the snow on Maurice's hair and face, Cubby thought Maurice was Santa.

"Ho ho ho," laughed Maurice. Outside, the horses shook and jingled their bells.

"It's Santa," Cubby whispered. "A *black* Santa."

Maurice just grinned. "Yup, you're right, it's me, Santa *Lemuel* Claus."

"I must be dreamin'," Cubby said, nodding back off to sleep.

Kris and Maurice quickly loaded the three boys onto the sled and wrapped them in blankets. Maurice backed into Crab Apple, who kicked him headfirst into the snow.

"Dangit, Crab Apple!" he shouted. Dangit the dog came running up, digging into the snow, trying to find his pants legs. "Sorry, Dangit, sorry! I didn't mean it!" Maurice said, kicking the dog away. With just his tail above the snow, Dangit found Maurice's pants leg and popped out of the snow with a pants leg in his mouth.

Kris looked at Maurice and said, "You and that dog do this often?"

"Too durn often," said Maurice. "Can't even use an innocent cuss word 'round here without that dog rippin' my pants up, leavin' me lookin' like some raggedy scarecrow."

With Crab Apple tied behind the sled they started back to the hotel. Maurice gazed at the kids and shook his head. "What are you goin' to do for toys, Santa?"

"Santa will think of somethin'. Don't you worry 'bout it."

"It's not me I'm worryin' 'bout. With the snow and all, ain't no one had time to do any shoppin'. Why, I sent for some perfume for my Eulla Mae, but the Sears wagon didn't never get here."

"Yes, it did," said Kris, pointing to the delivery wagon abandoned under the eaves of a barn.

"Well, I'll be," said Maurice. He hopped out and looked in the wagon. When the moon suddenly broke through the clouds, Maurice saw two large bags marked, Mansfield, Missouri. He hauled them to the sleigh.

"Don't suppose folks'd call that stealin'," Kris said.

"No, 'course not! I'm just goin' to leave it at the hotel," said Maurice, rummaging around in the bag. "Well, look here," he said, holding up a box. "It's marked *toys,* and addressed to Bedal's General Store."

"Santa always delivers," Kris chuckled, pulling off toward town.

As they entered the town, the two men began singing, "We Wish You a Merry Christmas." And faces peeked out from behind the snowy windows, wondering if it really was Santa going by.

CHAPTER 35

CHRISTMAS MORNING

anly's sleigh arrived in town right behind Maurice and Kris, so the hotel was the scene of a joyous reunion. The children were carried up to their beds, still asleep, and Martha and her two new babies were put in a warm room.

Rev. Youngun put the small, pink piglet into a box filled with rags, hid it in the barn, and put Dangit back in his cage. A small Christmas tree was brought in from the field, and they decorated it with popcorn and cranberries that Raul found in the kitchen.

With all the tales of the events of the past several days, no one noticed that Kris Kringle had slipped out before midnight. Laura and Manly stood by the front window and blinked their eyes as a brilliant flash of red blazed across the sky.

"What was that?" Manly asked. "A meteor?"

"I don't know," said Laura. "With everything that's happened, it could be anything."

They went back into the dining room and looked at the tree. Below it was a small wrapped box marked "Terry," one marked

"Mr. Johnson," and an envelope marked, "Open Christmas Morning."

"Who put these here?" Manly asked the people in the room. No one had noticed them before that moment.

Laura and Manly looked at each other and shook their heads. At the top of the stairs, Manly took Laura in his arms and kissed her. "Merry Christmas, Honeybee."

Christmas morning came early as the kids jumped out of bed, arguing whether the Santa they saw was black or white.

"I saw him!" He was a big black man with salt-and-pepper hair and beard. He ho-ho-hoed at me and said his name was . . ." Cubby paused, looking at Polly and Dr. George with pride, "said his name was Santa Lemuel Claus."

Larry spoke up. "It was the same white Santa that saved Terry at the bridge."

Sherry shook her head. "I saw Santa here at the hotel, and he was wearing his red long johns. He was a big white man."

"Who cares what color he is?" screamed Terry. Everyone in the room quieted down. "All I care 'bout is one thing."

"What's that?" laughed Dr. George.

"Did he bring me my present?" Terry asked, suddenly folding his arms and moaning. "Oh."

"What's wrong?" Larry asked.

"Got a stomachache," Terry said, trying to straighten up.

Cubby chuckled. "Serves you right for eatin' all that fudge."

"Let's go downstairs and see if Santa has presents for you children," Dr. George said, remembering the bag of Sears toys that Maurice had found. Before the words were out of his mouth, the kids were flying down the stairs. They stopped at the door and gazed at the Christmas tree.

"It's beautiful," Sherry whispered. "So beautiful."

"It thure ith," said Four-Eyes, standing behind her.

Laura and Manly came down and smiled. Manly said, "There's a box here for you, Mr. Johnson."

"There ith?" he exclaimed. "I knew Thanta wouldn't forget me."

He took the box from Manly and opened it. "My teeth! Thanta thure thame through!" He slipped the teeth in and wiggled his gums. "I knew Santa wouldn't forget me. All I asked for was my teeth, and he got 'em for me."

Terry saw the box marked with his name and ripped it open. "He got it! I knew he'd get it for me." He opened the blades of the pocketknife and proudly displayed them. "This one's even got a can opener."

Maurice handed Eulla Mae her perfume and gave each of the children a toy from the Sears bag. "I don't think Mr. Bedal will mind," he winked.

Laura picked up the letter marked "Open Christmas Morning" and read it:

Dear Good Neighbors:

You have shown me once again what Christmas is all about. By now you know that I got Mr. Johnson his teeth and the knife that Terry wanted.

Larry's present is out in the barn, and Cubby's present is already blossoming in the hearts of Doctor George and Polly.

Sherry's present was a little more difficult, but I think Rev. Youngun has gotten it for me.

It doesn't matter whether Santa's white, black, or polka dot, 'cause Santa's whatever you feel in your heart.

I will always treasure the memories of the Christmas I spent in Mansfield.

Kris Kringle

Laura let Manly and Dr. George read the letter. Maurice looked at it with Polly, Eulla Mae, and Rev. Youngun. Terry was wondering why the adults were sniffling, and Cubby, Larry, and Sherry were wondering where their presents were.

Four-Eyes came in, scratching his head. "Kris Kringle's checked out, but he didn't leave a trace. Room looks like it's never been slept in, and his name's not even on the register."

"He was here, all right," said Manly.

Rev. Youngun smiled. "Larry, you and Sherry got somethin' out in the barn."

The two children dashed out screaming as Dr. George looked up. He saw the mistletoe he and Polly were standing under and used his index finger to push Polly's chin up until she saw it. She giggled and closed her eyes. Maurice gave him a nudge. "Go on, kiss her. She loves you, I just know it."

As Dr. George and Polly kissed, Cubby smiled. "Oh Pops, this is great! I like Polly."

"So do I, son." Dr. George reached over and picked Cubby up. "I love you, Cubby. I'm goin' to be a good father to you."

"I love you, too, Pops."

Polly put her arms around them. "You're both standin' under the mistletoe, so give me a smooch."

Eulla Mae looked at Maurice, who was grinning like a schoolboy. "What you lookin' at? You ain't much of a hot lips yourself!"

She grabbed Maurice by the arm and dragged him over to the mistletoe. " 'Scuse me," she said, tapping Dr. George and Polly. "It's our turn."

By now, the rest of the hotel guests had come down the stairs, and they all applauded as Maurice and Eulla Mae kissed. Maurice pulled back, shaking his head. Eulla Mae laughed.

"What?" Maurice asked.

"I can see you blush," she whispered into his ear.

Rose came into the room. She pointed out the mistletoe to her father and mother and nudged them over, so Manly kissed Laura and everyone applauded again.

Lemuel, standing by the window, called Rose over. "Sh," he said, putting his finger to his lips. "See if you can hear it."

Rose leaned against the window and heard the soft jingling

of the bells, then looked up and saw a streak of red across the sky.

Lemuel nodded. "This is a very strange year." He took her hand. "Pinch me quick, so I can see if I'm still alive."

Soon Jacob came into the room, carrying the new babies. As he showed them off around the room, he walked over to Dr. George and asked Polly to hold the babies. "Doc, I want to thank you for what you've done. I was a darn fool. Can't say anythin' else, 'cept I'm sorry." Jacob stuck out his hand.

For a moment Dr. George looked at Jacob's extended hand, white and calloused. Then he reached out and shook it. "What did you name the boys?" he asked.

Martha and I named them Moses and Lemuel. Good family names," Jacob said, smiling.

Maurice and Dr. George smiled at each other and shrugged.

"Let me hold little Lemuel," Maurice said, taking the baby into his arms. "Lemuel! My, that's a good name."

Out in the barn, Larry stopped in his tracks when he saw the bow on the stall in front of his new horse. There was a note on the stall that read simply, "For Larry, from Santa."

Sherry looked around, hoping for her Christmas miracle. She was happy for Larry, but she had been praying that she would see. . . . Sherry stopped; she thought she'd heard a sound.

Sherry looked around again and heard the pig squeal again. When she glimpsed the pink ribbon, she ran over. Inside the rag-filled box was the cutest piglet in the whole world.

She picked it up and hugged it. Larry came over and picked up the card. "What's it say?" asked Sherry, tears in her eyes.

Larry opened it up. "It says 'Here's a little Bessie for Sherry. I love you. Santa.' "

"Oh, Bessie," Sherry said, kissing the pig and nuzzling it to her face. "I *knew* you'd come back!"

Laura stood in the doorway of the barn with Manly, Maurice, and Rev. Youngun.

Sherry ran up and stood in front of them. "Can you believe it? I've got my little Bessie!"

"Santa Claus is no myth, is he, Laura?" Manly asked, hugging her to him.

"All you have to do is believe," Laura smiled.

ABOUT THE AUTHOR

T. L. Tedrow is a best-selling author, screenwriter, and film producer. His books include the eight-book "Days of Laura Ingalls Wilder Series": *Missouri Homestead, Children of Promise, Good Neighbors, Home to the Prairie, The World's Fair, Mountain Miracle, The Great Debate,* and *Land of Promise,* which are the basis of a new television series. His four-book series on *The Younguns,* to be released in 1993, has also been sold as a television series. His first bestseller, *Death at Chappaquiddick,* has been made into a feature film. He lives with his wife, Carla, and four children in Winter Park, Florida.